Tricks of the Trade

Lorenzo, the magician, held the third knife up to the audience. "Here comes the tricky part. I'm going to aim this knife directly above Larissa's head. Ready?" he asked his assistant. Larissa nodded.

"One." Lorenzo paused and drew the knife back. "Two." He took aim. "Three!"

But as soon as the magician said "Three," and let go of the knife, Frank had a terrible feeling in the pit of his stomach.

From where he stood, it looked as if Lorenzo's throw was off. The knife *was* headed right for Larissa.

But this time it wasn't going to miss.

The Hardy Boys Mystery Stories

Available from MINSTREL Books

104

The

HARDY BOYS®

TRICKS OF THE TRADE

FRANKLIN W. DIXON

A MINSTREL® BOOK

PUBLISHED BY POCKET BOOKS

New York   London   Toronto   Sydney   Tokyo   Singapore

A MINSTREL PAPERBACK *ORIGINAL*

A Minstrel Book published by
POCKET BOOKS, a division of Simon & Schuster Inc.
1230 Avenue of the Americas, New York, NY 10020

Copyright © 1990 by Simon & Schuster Inc.
Cover artwork copyright © 1990 by Paul Bachem
Produced by Mega-Books of New York, Inc.

ISBN: 0-671-69273-9

First Minstrel Books printing October 1990

10 9 8 7 6 5 4 3 2 1

THE HARDY BOYS MYSTERY STORIES is a trademark of Simon & Schuster Inc.

THE HARDY BOYS, A MINSTREL BOOK and colophon are registered trademarks of Simon & Schuster Inc.

Printed in the U.S.A.

Contents

1 Ladies and Gentlemen— Lorenzo the Magnificent!

"Wow! I can't believe it!" Chet Morton shouted over the noise of honking car horns. "I'm actually going to see Lorenzo the Magnificent in person! And watch him do all his famous magic tricks!"

Frank Hardy reached out to help his friend Chet Morton lift a bulging duffel bag out of a taxi and over to a hotel bellhop. "The way you've been practicing, Chet," he told him, "Lorenzo better watch out for the competition!"

"Frank's right," Joe said, his amusement evident in his blue eyes. "You haven't stopped working on your rope tricks since we left Bayport."

Frank knew that Chet sometimes let a new hobby take over his life. Then, a week later, he'd

1

usually forget about it. This time, though, Chet's interest in magic had lasted at least two weeks, ever since he heard that Lorenzo the Magnificent was coming to New York City.

The three boys followed the bellhop through the crowded and expensive-looking hotel lobby. Chet stopped to pull some string out of his pocket. "Wait, there's one I forgot to show you," he started to say.

"Later, Chet," said Frank. "Right now I think we'd better check in." He glanced at his watch and checked the sign on the hotel registration desk. It listed the day's schedule of events. "It's almost time for Lorenzo's first show."

"You're right," Chet agreed. "Come on, let's hurry up. I don't want to miss a minute."

Frank shook his head and ran his hand through his dark hair. His brown eyes reflected the humor he saw in Chet's enthusiasm. He exchanged a knowing glance with his brother, both of them realizing they would have to put up with Chet's excitement for the weekend. Lorenzo was going to be holding seminars, too, and Chet was totally psyched to learn just how the magician managed to do his tricks.

Usually Frank and Joe Hardy were busy solving mysteries, tracking down villains and cracking cases that sometimes stumped even the local police. The Hardys hadn't had a case in a while, and

Frank thought coming to New York with Chet would be a good way for him and Joe to spend the weekend.

"I don't know, Frank," Joe said as he signed the hotel register and took the keys the clerk handed him. "Chet's really gone overboard this time. I've never seen him as into anything as he is with this."

Chet was standing off to the side, reading his book of magic tricks. "Hey, Frank, Joe," he called out. "I just realized what I was doing wrong with the 'vanishing knot.' It says here—"

"You can show us later, Chet," Frank told him. "We should drop our bags off before the show starts."

"Right," said Chet. He stuffed his book back in his pocket. "Let's go."

After the boys put their bags in their room, they headed back downstairs to the hotel banquet room where Lorenzo would perform his opening act. Already the banquet room was filling up with well-dressed grown-ups and excited kids. They found seats toward the back of the crowded room. Joe was six feet tall, and his brother was an inch taller, so they were both able to see over the crowd. Chet, however, was having difficulty seeing over the man in front of him.

"We should have gotten here earlier," Chet grumbled.

3

"But, Chet, you were the one—" Joe started to say.

"Sure, blame it on me," Chet said. "It's because of you that we missed the earlier train." With that, Chet took out a handkerchief and a shoelace.

"Now, look," he told the Hardys. "It's all in keeping your attention off what I'm doing." Frank noticed that the shoelace was tied in a loop and had a lot of knots at one end. In the middle of the loop was another, looser knot.

Chet put the handkerchief over the shoelace. "Hold on to the ends of the shoelace," he told Joe. "You know," he said, moving his hands under the handkerchief, "I just can't figure out why this trick doesn't work."

Frank watched as Chet made a face. Joe rolled his eyes at his older brother. Chet had been trying to get the trick right for the last half hour of their train ride from Bayport.

"If I just . . ." Chet moved his hands some more under the handkerchief. He made another face. "I think I tied these knots too tight," he told Joe.

Frank knew that the point of the trick was to make it seem as if the knot in the middle of the loop of shoelace had "disappeared." But he also knew that all Chet was doing was pulling on the loop to make the loose knot become just another one of the knots at the end of the loop. It didn't take a genius to figure it out.

4

"There!" Chet said triumphantly. Sure enough, when he yanked the handkerchief away, the knot in the middle of the loop of shoelace had "disappeared."

Joe counted off the knots at the end of the shoelace. "Five," he declared. "There were only four before, Chet. I counted."

Chet playfully knocked Joe's head away, messing up his blond hair. "Come on, you only really know because I explained it before. This time my patter was good enough that it was distracting you from the trick." .

Frank smiled. "Patter?"

"That's what magicians use to take your attention away from the trick. They explain it right here—"

Chet had pulled his magic book out of his pocket and was turning the pages. But before he could find the spot he was looking for, the lights had begun to dim, and dry ice was filling a stage that had been set up at one end of the room. The crowd hushed and a booming voice came over the PA system.

"Ladies and gentlemen," the voice said in low tones. "It is my pleasure to give you . . . Lorenzo the Magnificent!"

A flash of bright light momentarily blinded the audience. After it faded, Frank saw a figure in a black cape standing on the stage. "Over the next

5

several days," Lorenzo intoned, "you will see amazing feats of magic. Like this."

With that, the magician flung his cape back and threw his hands out to one side. Bright light flashed again, and when it was gone, a tall woman in a red sequined costume was standing next to the magician. She smiled and tossed back her long, dark hair. Frank looked at Joe and saw his brother's eyes widen at the sight of the magician's beautiful assistant.

The crowd clapped. "My assistant, the Mysterious Larissa," Lorenzo said. Larissa took a bow.

"But that's just the beginning," Lorenzo said, tossing his cape into Larissa's arms.

"Wow," Chet whispered. "Isn't he great?"

Frank had to admit his friend was right. With his tuxedo and slightly graying hair, Lorenzo looked distinguished and dramatic. When he smiled, Frank could see his white teeth flashing, even from where they sat. The magician truly did have an amazing presence.

"You've seen magicians pull things out of hats," Lorenzo told the crowd. He laughed and the crowd laughed along with him. "But watch carefully while I pull things out of Larissa's hat."

Frank watched the magician's assistant put on a large black hat and stand with her hands on her hips as she faced the audience. There was a silly, bored expression on her face.

6

Lorenzo knocked lightly on the top of the hat, then faced the audience, looking confused. "This trick usually works," he confessed.

Larissa leaned over to whisper in his ear. "Of course," Lorenzo said, shaking his head. "How could I have forgotten?"

He rapped on the hat again, three times this time. "There's a secret code," he explained to the audience. With that, the hat popped open and three doves flew out of it.

"Pretty clever," Frank admitted with a laugh.

An assistant wheeled out a ten-foot-tall cylindrical tube made out of glass. "This is the trick Lorenzo is known for," Chet told Frank and Joe. "He chains himself upside down inside the tube and still manages to escape! The guy is amazing!"

Chet craned his neck to see over the rows of people in front of them while Lorenzo climbed a ladder the assistant had placed against the tube. Larissa climbed up after him and helped Lorenzo lock his ankles into what looked like handcuffs attached to a metal bar.

"That looks painful," Joe whispered to Chet.

Chet nodded. "That's what I thought when I first heard about the trick. But they're special handcuffs—I think they're called 'stocks.' They're made out of rubber so they don't hurt."

"I always remind him to be careful," Larissa told the audience as she finished locking

7

Lorenzo's ankles into the cuffs and pocketed the key.

"But just in case," she continued with a smile, "I also give Lorenzo a farewell kiss." With that, she leaned over to kiss Lorenzo before he lowered himself, head first, into the tube.

Frank found himself paying close attention, along with the rest of the crowd. Larissa came down the ladder and pressed a button on the side of the tube. Soon, the tube was filling up with dry ice.

"This is too cool." Joe leaned over to whisper to his brother. "You know it can't be easy for him to see what he's doing with all that dry ice swirling around him."

"Or for us," Frank added. "That's some smoke screen!"

"Hey," Chet said in a loud whisper. "I can't pay attention to what Larissa's doing with you guys talking so much."

"Sorry, Chet," Frank told his friend. He went back to watching Lorenzo's assistant. She was down in the front row of the audience now.

"What's she doing?" Joe asked his brother.

Frank shook his head. "I can't tell from here."

A kid in the front row started laughing, and Larissa held a rabbit up for the audience to see.

"I bet Chet wishes he could be up there, watching Larissa," Joe said as their heavyset

8

friend squirmed in his seat, trying to see through the sea of heads in front of them.

"You bet I do," Chet cracked, twisting around in his seat. "I know I should have gotten my mom to drive us to the train station. That van of yours—"

"Hey, Chet," said Frank. His eyes were on the stage.

"Yeah?"

"If you stopped talking for a minute, you might see something really interesting."

Onstage, the top of the cylindrical tube was slowly opening. Then, in one swift move, Lorenzo the Magnificent hoisted himself up, head first, out of the tube.

Triumphantly, he lifted up the pole to show the audience that the two cuffs that had held his ankles were now open. "I guess the farewell kiss was premature," he jokingly told the crowd.

Larissa came bounding back onstage and took Lorenzo's hand. The two magicians bowed as the audience burst into thunderous applause.

"Wow!" Chet was shaking his head in disbelief. "How did he do it?"

Frank lifted his eyebrows. "You got me, Chet. I guess we'll just have to attend his seminars to find out."

"You don't think he's going to give away his secrets, do you?" Joe asked. "I have a feeling the seminars are going to make Lorenzo seem even more magnificent."

"Magicians don't usually like too many people to know just how they do their tricks," Chet agreed.

Frank looked around the banquet room to see what other tricks were in store for them. Ushers were passing out small white boxes to the audience, while Larissa and Lorenzo were handing out the same kind of boxes to people in the front row. When Frank, Joe, and Chet got theirs, they saw the boxes contained trick handcuffs.

"Now, don't try this at home," Lorenzo joked as Larissa put a set of handcuffs on his wrists. Around them, many people in the crowd put the cuffs on, too.

"The trick to using these," the magician explained, "is all in the wrist."

Frank watched the magician move his hands together three times. Some people in the audience imitated him. On the third pass, Lorenzo shouted, "Now," and pulled his wrists apart. The handcuffs snapped open and fell to the floor.

Around the audience there were groans of frustration and some shouts of triumph as people tried to snap their handcuffs open.

Lorenzo let out a booming laugh. "Try again!" he urged them. "One, two." He paused. "Remember to snap your wrist. Three!"

More people in the audience managed to get their cuffs open. Around Frank, a few people kept trying and finally managed to snap their wrists free.

Then Frank heard one voice, a woman's, above the noisy crowd.

"My bracelet! My diamond bracelet!" she screamed. "It's gone!"

2 The Joke's on Joe

"Come on, Frank, let's go!" Joe Hardy rushed up toward the front of the room, with his brother and Chet close behind.

A crowd had gathered around a well-dressed, blond-haired woman in an expensive green suit and black high heels. Sapphire earrings glistened from under her short, stylish haircut. A blond boy who looked as if he might be her son stood at her side, his blue eyes blinking with surprise. Lorenzo and Larissa were there, too.

"Of course I'm sure I had it," the woman was telling the group. "Oh, this is just terrible." She put her hands to her face and started to cry. The boy pulled on the woman's green jacket and said, "Don't cry, Mom."

12

"Excuse me," Joe said, stepping up to the group. "Maybe we can help."

"Help?" the woman asked, lowering her hands and taking a look at Joe. She obviously wasn't impressed with what she saw. "What makes you think you can help?"

"Well—" Joe began.

"I'm Frank Hardy," Frank introduced himself. "And this is my brother, Joe, and our friend Chet. Joe and I are amateur detectives."

"Frank and Joe have actually solved a lot of mysteries," Chet added. "They might be able to help you find your bracelet."

Several people in the crowd had given up searching under the folding chairs and were listening to the conversation.

"Let them take a shot at it, ma'am," Lorenzo told the woman politely. His intense yellowish brown eyes showed an honest interest. "I'm afraid we have to go now, but I certainly hope you find your bracelet," he added.

Larissa gave the woman a concerned look and went off with the magician. The crowd murmured, and several people followed the magicians, hoping to get autographs. Joe watched Lorenzo leave and noticed that Larissa stayed off to the side. She was avoiding the rest of the crowd as she talked to a young man in a business suit.

13

The crowd around the blond woman and her son started to thin out. Most of them seemed to have lost interest in the missing bracelet.

"Why don't you tell us what happened, Mrs. . . . I'm sorry, I didn't get your name," said Joe politely.

"It's Mrs. Sampson, Irene Sampson." The woman offered her hand, and Joe shook it.

"Nice to meet you, Mrs. Sampson," said Frank, shaking her hand next. "Is this your son?" He gestured to the boy, who looked to be about ten years old, standing next to Irene Sampson.

"Yes. This is Mike," she told them. "He loves magic. That's why he came with me."

"Isn't Lorenzo the greatest?" Mike asked.

"You bet," Chet agreed.

"Even my mom was having a great time. Until the handcuff trick." Mike bit his lip.

"Is that when you noticed your bracelet was missing?" Joe asked.

Irene Sampson nodded. "I let Mike put the handcuffs on me, but when I snapped them open, I realized my bracelet was gone." Tears started coming to her pale blue eyes. "That bracelet has been in my family for years. It was my great-grandmother's. It's priceless. And now it's gone!"

"Let's take a look around, Frank," Joe suggested.

"Right," Frank agreed.

14

With Chet's help, Frank and Joe searched under the seats. Joe figured the bracelet probably had flown off Mrs. Sampson's wrist when she'd tried to get out of the trick handcuffs. It had to be nearby.

But ten minutes later the boys had finished searching the whole room while Mike and his mother looked on. They came up empty-handed.

"I'm afraid you're right, Mrs. Sampson," Joe told the woman. "It looks like your bracelet is gone."

"Are you sure you were wearing it this afternoon?" Frank asked.

Irene Sampson nodded. "I'm positive. I remember because I put it on just before Mike and I left our room. And the woman sitting next to me complimented me on it after we sat down."

"Since we didn't find it here, and you know you had it when you came into the room, it looks like it might have been stolen," said Joe. "Maybe it did fall off when you tried to snap open the handcuffs."

"And maybe someone found it and walked off with it," Chet concluded.

Frank nodded. "Could be. Mike, did you notice your mom's bracelet when you put the handcuffs on her?"

Mike shook his head. "I don't think so. But I wasn't really looking for it," he admitted.

"I'm sure your friend Chet is right. And I'm

15

going to report this to the hotel security right away," Irene Sampson said with determination. "Come on, Mike."

She grabbed her son's hand and started for the exit. Joe followed her, with Frank and Chet close behind. They went downstairs from the banquet room to the hotel lobby. There, Mrs. Sampson asked a hotel clerk, whose badge read "George," to get the manager.

"I want to report a theft," she said firmly.

The young clerk's freckled face turned a bit red. "A th-th-theft?" he stammered. "Here at the hotel?"

Joe nodded. "Could you call the manager, please?"

George nodded. "Sure thing," he said, and placed the call. "Miss Bern will be right down. She's the manager," he explained. "In the meantime, is there anything I can do?" He nervously ran his hands through his curly red hair.

"That's okay," Joe said. "We'll wait for Miss Bern."

Within a few minutes, Joe spotted a tall, dark-haired woman wearing a red suit come through a door behind the hotel's front desk. Two men were with her. The younger one was tall, well-built, and had sandy blond hair. The older one was middle-aged and distinguished, and he was wearing a conservative gray suit.

16

"I'm Nina Bern," the hotel manager said as she smoothed her skirt. "This is Clyde Spector, head of security." The younger of the two men nodded.

Joe wasn't sure, but he thought he recognized the guy from somewhere. Then he realized that the man looked a lot like the guy he'd seen Larissa talking to just a few minutes earlier in the banquet room.

"And Nat Dietrich, my assistant," Nina Bern went on, introducing the other man. Joe introduced himself, Frank, and Chet. Then he told the hotel manager that Irene Sampson's bracelet had disappeared.

Dietrich nodded and reached out to shake Irene Sampson's hand. "George told us you wanted to report a theft. Just what happened?" he asked with authority.

"Mrs. Sampson is missing an antique diamond bracelet," Joe told the man.

Dietrich gave them all a keen look and rubbed his chin thoughtfully. "I'm very sorry. We'll certainly do our best to help you find it."

Clyde Spector took a slim notebook out of his jacket pocket and started writing. "When did you notice it was missing?" he asked.

"Right at the end of the magic show," Mike Sampson put in. "That's when my mom realized it wasn't on her wrist."

Joe explained how they had looked for the bracelet under the seats, but hadn't found it.

"I think it was stolen," Chet added. "Otherwise, why didn't it turn up?"

"It may well have been," Spector said, looking up from the notes he was taking. "We'll report the theft to the police, but—I might suggest, Mrs. Sampson—you could be wrong. Why don't you check your room, then give me a call, okay?"

Irene Sampson looked flustered. "I told you, I'm sure I was wearing it."

"Of course," Dietrich said. He took her arm and started ushering Irene and Mike to the elevators. "Miss Bern and I will do our best to help you find it. You can be assured of that."

"Meanwhile," Nina Bern added, "you should report this to your insurance company. I assume the bracelet was insured?"

Irene Sampson nodded. "I'll do that right away."

Joe shot Frank a questioning look. The hotel management didn't seem too eager to help Irene Sampson out.

Frank nodded in understanding and turned to the hotel manager. "Miss Bern," he said, "we really should call the police right away. I hate to say this, but one of your guests could be a thief."

Nina Bern sighed. "You're right, of course. I'll go call them now." She stepped back behind the desk. "If you don't mind, though," she added before leaving them, "I'd appreciate it if you kept this to yourselves. The publicity would be just awful for the hotel." She reached up to smooth her jet black hair. "I'm sure you understand," she added with a questioning look.

"Sure," Joe said. "No problem."

"Good. Please keep me posted, Mrs. Sampson," Nina told the woman. "Here's my office number." She handed Irene a card, and nodded to Dietrich and Spector. "I'll be in my office if you need me."

"Thanks for your help," Irene Sampson said to the Hardys after Nina Bern had gone. Then she took Mike's hand and headed for the elevators.

"We'll do our best to help you," Clyde Spector called after Mrs. Sampson. Joe didn't think he sounded very reassuring. "I think you kids should leave this to us," Spector told Joe and Frank after the Sampsons had gotten into the elevator.

"But—" Joe began.

"Come on, Joe," Chet said. "Let's go get some dinner. I'm starving, and it doesn't look like these guys want us around."

Dietrich put his hand on Joe's shoulder. "We can handle this problem, Joe. Not that we don't appreciate what you did. But there were a lot of people in that room. Anyone could have taken the bracelet. This kind of thing happens."

"Sure," Joe muttered.

19

"Mr. Dietrich's right, Joe," Frank said. "And I'm pretty hungry myself." He signaled Joe with his eyes and mouthed, "Later."

"There's a coffee shop right here in the lobby," Dietrich told them. "Dinner's on the hotel. Just a little 'thank you' for what you did."

"Thanks," Joe said abruptly, "but I'll pay for myself."

"What's gotten into you?" Frank asked his brother when they were sitting down in the hotel's coffee shop. Chet had ordered a hamburger deluxe with a chocolate shake, and Frank and Joe had both asked for cheeseburgers. "I could tell you didn't like that guy, but he did offer to pay for our dinner. Mom would say you were rude."

"Rude, schmude. He was the one who didn't want our help," Joe said, taking a sip of his soda.

"He sure did give us the brush-off," Chet agreed. "And neither one of them seemed to want to do too much about Mrs. Sampson's missing bracelet."

"Well," Frank started, "Dietrich was right. There were a lot of people there."

"Baloney!" Joe interrupted. "They just don't want to deal with the fact that one of their guests might be a thief. They should question everyone who was at the show."

"That would be hard," Frank pointed out, as the

20

waitress brought their burgers. "Considering that no one even knows who was there."

Chet popped several french fries into his mouth. He wiped his hand on his napkin and said, still chewing, "I want to check out these handcuffs. With all the commotion, I didn't even get the chance to try mine."

He pulled the set of trick handcuffs out of his pocket. "Who wants to be the lucky one? Frank?"

Frank shook his head. "No thanks, Chet. I'd rather use my hands to eat this burger." He picked up his cheeseburger and took a huge bite.

"Joe?"

Joe looked at his friend. "Huh?" he asked. "Sorry, I wasn't listening."

"I said I think you should try these on for size. See what it feels like to be on the other side." Chet laughed, and before Joe could stop him, Chet had grabbed his wrists.

"Wait a minute, Chet," Joe said, trying to stop him. It was too late. Chet had snapped the cuffs shut.

"Now pull them apart, like this." Chet imitated Lorenzo. "One, two, and on three, snap them open."

Joe shook his head and rolled his eyes. "I don't know, Chet. The things you do for your friends."

"Ready?" Chet asked. "One."

21

Joe moved his wrists apart, then back together. "Two."

He pulled them apart again.

"Three!"

Joe yanked the cuffs apart, expecting them to snap open. Instead, the metal rings dug into his wrists.

"Try it again," Chet urged, looking a little worried.

Joe tried again, but it was no use. The cuffs held. And he was stuck!

3 Nothing up His Sleeve

"Hey, Chet," Joe Hardy exclaimed. "You'd better do something about this!" He struggled once more to get the handcuffs open.

Between bursts of laughter, Frank managed to say, "That's about the funniest thing I've seen today."

Chet laughed just as hard. "It sure is," he agreed. Seeing the look on Joe's face, though, was almost enough to quiet both Chet and Frank.

"It's not funny," Joe insisted. "In fact, do you think one of you could stop laughing long enough to help me out here?" Joe looked at the handcuffs carefully, trying to see if they had gotten jammed somehow. But everything seemed to be normal.

"Let me try," Frank offered. He reached into his back pocket for the penknife he usually carried. "Maybe I can pry them open."

"Good luck," Joe told him. "If these cuffs are anything like the real thing, we'll be here all night."

"They're trick handcuffs, Joe," Chet reminded him.

"Yeah, some trick!" Joe looked at Chet and said, "Now would be a great time to use some of that magic you've been studying. If I'm still wearing these on Sunday . . ."

"Sorry," Chet grumbled. "You might think I planned this, the way you're acting."

"Easy, guys," Frank said, looking up from the cuffs. "Can I have a little quiet here? I'm trying to concentrate."

Joe looked on while Frank worked at the lock on the right handcuff. His brother was usually an ace at lock-picking, but this one seemed to be giving him trouble.

Frank shook his head. "I don't know what's wrong, Joe, but I can't seem to get it open."

"Is everything okay? What seems to be the problem?" a familiar voice asked.

Joe glanced up to see Clyde Spector coming over to their table.

"Need some help, boys?" the security guard asked, standing next to their table.

"Well, Mr. Spector," Frank told him, "we just might. My brother Joe's kind of stuck in these handcuffs."

Spector raised an eyebrow. "What in the world are you doing with handcuffs on?" he asked.

"It's a long story," Joe said. "Right now, all I want to do is get them off."

Spector smiled. "Lost the key, eh?" he asked. "That happens. It's pretty embarrassing, though. In fact, the very first time I used handcuffs—"

"There isn't a key," Chet said, interrupting him.

"No key?" Spector asked curiously. "I hate to ask, but did you know there wasn't a key when you put them on, Joe?"

Joe snorted. "Of course I knew. I'm not stupid."

"These are trick handcuffs," Frank explained. "You're not supposed to need a key."

"I see." He took a look at Frank's penknife, which was lying on the table next to their now-cold burgers. "Couldn't pick it, either?" Frank shook his head. Chet explained to Spector that Lorenzo had given out the handcuffs at his performance that afternoon. "Maybe Lorenzo's got a key," Chet suggested.

"Good thinking," Clyde agreed. "But let me see if I can get them open first."

Frank handed him the penknife. Joe held out his wrists, and Spector stuck a blade into the lock on the right cuff. At first the blade slipped, but

25

then, with one quick movement, Clyde had the lock open. The left one took even less time. Chet let out a big sigh of relief.

"Gee, thanks," Joe said, rubbing his wrists. "For a minute there, I thought I'd have to sleep in these things."

"How'd you do it?" Frank asked. "I mean, why didn't it work when I tried it?"

Clyde picked up the cuffs from where they'd fallen onto the table. "Because the locks were jammed. You need to know what you're doing to get it open."

"But how did you know?" Chet asked, looking at the handcuffs curiously.

Spector smiled. "I've had friends who were into magic," he explained. "That's why I'm planning on catching Lorenzo's shows, too. I missed his opening act, but I can't wait for the show tonight. Want to see a trick?"

Joe groaned. "Not another one!" he said.

But Chet was eager to see what the security guard could do. "We'd love to!" he told Clyde.

"Why not?" Frank agreed. Spector sat down at the table, and the three boys pulled up their chairs.

"This one is really quite simple," Clyde told them. He cleared a space next to the edge of the table. "You still want this burger?" he asked Chet.

Chet gulped, looking at all the wasted food. "I guess not," he said.

Clyde motioned for the waitress to come over. Once she had cleared away the plates, Spector placed a coin on the table. "Now pay attention. The quarter is head side up, right?" The three boys nodded. "Watch carefully," he told them. With that, he placed the saltshaker over the coin. "I'm going to cover the shaker and make the coin turn over."

Chet started to ask a question, but Clyde motioned for him to be quiet and watch. Spector took a napkin and covered the shaker. "Just to be on the safe side," he told them, "I'm going to cover it again."

He took another napkin and covered the shaker a second time. "Now, I think we should check that coin one more time, don't you?"

Chet nodded. Frank and Joe exchanged a quizzical look. Joe kept his eyes peeled on Spector. He wasn't going to let his attention get diverted.

The quarter was still head side up. Spector put the saltshaker back on top of the coin. Then, in a flash, he slammed his hand down on top of it. The napkin crumpled under the blow. The shaker was gone!

"How'd you—?" Chet asked, baffled.

Joe lifted the napkin. Sure enough, the shaker

27

was gone, although the coin was still there. Now it was tail side up. He let out a laugh. "Pretty neat!" he admitted.

Frank wanted to know how Spector had done the trick, but the security guard wouldn't tell them. Instead, Spector reached his hand inside his jacket pocket. "I think I should leave this behind," he told them with a smile. He took out the saltshaker. "Wouldn't want to be accused of stealing from the hotel, would I?"

The three boys laughed in unison. "Guess not," Frank agreed.

Spector stood up. "Well, gotta run. See you boys later."

"Hey," Joe said. "Thanks for your help."

"Amazing," Chet said, shaking his head after Spector had left. "I've got to practice that one."

"How about practicing in the room?" Frank suggested, calling the waitress over for the check. "I'd like to rest up before Lorenzo's performance tonight."

The three boys were heading out of the coffee shop and into the lobby when Chet spotted Larissa walking toward the elevators. Joe caught the look of awe in Chet's eyes as his friend ran across the lobby. Chet was totally starstruck.

"Excuse me," Chet called out to Larissa. "Um—I hate to bother you, but could I have your autograph?" Chet pulled his magic book out of his pocket. Frank and Joe stood close behind Chet.

Up close, Joe thought that Larissa was even prettier than she appeared onstage. She had changed from her sequined gown into a simple outfit of jeans, a red T-shirt, and a pair of cowboy boots.

Larissa's gray eyes took in the three boys. "Sure," she agreed in a friendly voice. Then she pulled a pen out from behind Chet's ear. "Is this color okay?"

Chet laughed while Frank and Joe shook their heads. "I can see people are going to be pulling things out of thin air a lot this weekend," Joe said with a laugh.

Larissa signed Chet's book. While he was thanking her and telling her how much he admired her, Larissa stood by with a shy smile on her pretty face. "Thanks," she said. "I hope you enjoy the show tonight."

"Oh, we will," Chet told her. "We're just going up to our room now. But we're going to get there early to make sure we've got good seats. Right?" he asked Joe.

"Right, Chet," Joe said.

"If you're going up to your room, don't you think you'll be needing your key?" Larissa asked. With that, she pulled their room key out of her pants pocket.

"What?" Frank checked his pockets. Sure enough, their room key was gone. "How'd you—?"

Before Larissa could answer him, Nat Dietrich came over to where the group was standing. "We've notified the police," he told them. "They're sending a detective over." He paused.

"And?" Joe asked.

Dietrich couldn't take his eyes off Larissa. "And . . . I'm sorry," he said to the magician. "I don't think we've met. My name is Nat Dietrich. I'm the assistant manager of the Hotel Regency."

Larissa smiled and held out her hand. "Larissa Rovitch," she said. "I'm with Lorenzo the Magnificent. The magician."

"Of course," Dietrich said.

"Mr. Dietrich," Frank said, interrupting them. "Just what did the police say?"

"Pretty much what I told you," the assistant manager said, finally taking his eyes off Larissa. "That with so many people in the room, it's going to be very hard to track down the thief."

"Are you talking about the missing bracelet?" Larissa asked in a soft voice. When Dietrich nodded, Larissa shook her head sadly. "Such a shame. But jewelry is quite easy to lose," she added.

"True. That's what I was trying to tell these boys." Dietrich motioned to Frank, Joe, and Chet.

30

"They seem to think they can help the woman find her bracelet, but I'm afraid it's probably lost."

Frank and Joe looked at each other. Chet shrugged his shoulders. Joe was ready to tell Dietrich they weren't giving up on finding the bracelet when the elevator doors next to them opened up.

"Look," Chet said in a loud whisper. "It's Lorenzo!"

Sure enough, the tall figure stepping out of the elevator was none other than Lorenzo the Magnificent. He had changed out of his tuxedo into a pair of chinos and a white shirt, but Frank thought the magician still looked impressive. Up close, his handsome features and graying temples made him look even more distinguished.

"Larissa!" Lorenzo called out in a deep voice. "I was looking for you."

"I was on my way up when I ran into these boys and Mr. Dietrich," Larissa explained. "He was telling us about the theft that happened earlier today."

"I'm so sorry it had to disturb your performance—" Dietrich began, putting a comforting arm around Larissa's shoulders.

What happened next surprised everyone.

"You!" Lorenzo shouted as he lunged for Dietrich, grabbing his lapels and pulling the man toward him. "Keep your hands off her. Or else!"

31

4 Mesmerized by Magic

"What!" Dietrich shook himself free and held his hands up to defend himself. "This man's a lunatic!"

Frank meanwhile had reacted in a flash and was pushing Lorenzo back. As the magician let his slender hands drop to his sides, Frank was sure he saw a look of pure hatred come over the man's face. What was that all about? Frank wondered.

"Just stay away from her," Lorenzo warned again. With that, he pushed his way through the hotel lobby and stormed out into the street.

Dietrich blew out a deep breath, then turned to Larissa. "Are you all right?" he asked. Frank thought the concern in Dietrich's voice was more than friendly.

"I'm fine," Larissa told him, pushing her hair back over her ears.

"Has this kind of thing happened before?" Frank asked.

"Never," she said with a confused look on her face. "Probably the pressure from performing so much is getting to him. Right now, though, I have to get ready for tonight's performance. See you there?" she asked.

"Sure," Joe said. "Take it easy, okay?"

Larissa nodded and got into a waiting elevator.

"I'll let you know if the police can tell us anything," Dietrich informed them after Larissa had gone. "But—"

"I know," said Frank. "Don't expect anything, right?"

"Right," Dietrich agreed.

"Look, Mr. Dietrich," Joe put in, "there must be a list somewhere of everyone who was at that performance. We could question people. See if anyone saw anything."

"Joe's got a point, Mr. Dietrich," Chet said. "We were sitting too far back to see anything, but maybe someone sitting near Mrs. Sampson saw the thief pocket her bracelet."

Nat Dietrich sighed. "You kids don't seem to

understand. Most of the people in the front rows of that audience have a lot of money. They're here because the hotel invited them."

Frank gave the man a questioning look. "Why did the hotel invite them?"

"Because the Hotel Regency is being evaluated by the American Hotel Association and its members," Dietrich explained. "That means prominent hotel people are staying here. In fact, Lorenzo is our special attraction this weekend, and we don't want anything to interfere with our guests having the best time possible at his performances."

"Even if it means covering up a theft?" Joe asked, stunned.

"We're not covering it up," Dietrich insisted. "The police have been called in. Mrs. Sampson has notified her insurance company. We'll have extra security at future performances. Clyde Spector has assured me of that."

"You're doing everything you can," Frank concluded. "That's what you're telling us."

"Exactly." Dietrich reached out to shake their hands. "Now I'm afraid I must be off, too. It's a very hectic weekend for us, as I'm sure you understand."

Chet checked his watch. "Look at the time. We have to get going, too."

"Mr. Dietrich, just one more thing," Joe said. Frank watched his brother put on his most charming smile. "Isn't there any way we could see a list of who was in the audience at that performance?"

"Impossible," Dietrich asserted firmly. "I simply cannot violate the privacy of my guests that way. They're too important. It would be insulting for them to be accused of theft!"

Frank grabbed Joe's arm. "Mr. Dietrich has a point, Joe. Come on." He dragged his brother into an open elevator nearby.

When the doors had closed, Joe turned to Frank. "What's wrong with that guy?" he asked again.

"Nothing's wrong with him," Frank told his brother. "You didn't like him the first time you met him, and now you're trying to find another excuse not to like him."

"He's just doing his job," Chet added with a shrug. "Personally, I can see his point."

"We'll see what happens tonight," Joe said.

"Look, Joe," Frank said as the elevator stopped at their floor. "There's no reason to think anything else is going to be stolen. And maybe Irene Sampson will even find her bracelet."

"Sure, Frank," Joe said. "And Clyde Spector really did make that saltshaker disappear."

* * *

35

The New York City skyline shone with a dazzling number of lights as Frank, Joe, and Chet entered the restaurant on top of the World Trade Center later that night. Inside the restaurant, Frank scanned the crowd of expensively dressed guests. Waiters were serving champagne and hors d'oeuvres—even caviar, Frank noticed.

"The hotel really went all out on this one," Chet whispered.

Frank nodded, feeling a little underdressed in his suit compared to all the men in tuxedos. "They even catered this themselves. While I was waiting in the lobby for you and Joe, George told me that Nina Bern had her whole kitchen staff come over here to prepare the food. She really wants to impress these people with what the hotel can do."

"Well, I think we should take advantage of the situation," Chet said, heading over to the buffet.

"Frank," Joe said, helping himself to the shrimp, "there's Irene Sampson."

Frank spied Irene Sampson and her son, Mike, who looked a little uncomfortable in his suit and tie, talking to Clyde Spector. Standing with them was an older woman, who had her hand on Irene's arm and seemed to be trying to reassure her.

"Frank, Joe, oh, and Chet, too," Irene called out when she saw the boys. "Mr. Spector says the police can't do a thing." Even through her make-up, Frank could see the woman was still upset.

36

"That's too bad," Frank said with a sigh. "Is there anything we can do, Clyde?" he asked the security guard.

Clyde shook his head. "Dietrich doesn't want to question the guests—not even on the sly—so I suppose not."

"It's just a terrible thing to have happened, Irene," the woman standing next to Mrs. Sampson said, shaking her head.

"This is Katherine Hammond," Irene said. "Katherine and I are on the board of the American Hotel Association."

"What's the board going to do about this?" Joe asked.

Katherine Hammond shook her graying head again. Emeralds sparkled at her ears, and her voice had a brassy, businesslike tone. "These things happen. We know the hotel is doing what it can. We can't really expect the hotel people to question our own members, after all."

Frank exchanged a look with Joe, raising his eyebrows. "Then there's really nothing we can do," he told Mrs. Sampson.

Spector nodded and answered for her. "I'm afraid that's true." He ran his hands through his blond hair. "If you'll excuse me, I have to supervise the other guards now. We've put extra people on for the night."

"Dietrich told us," said Frank. "I guess we should sit down now."

"Sounds good to me," Chet agreed, obviously anxious to get a good seat this time. He picked an hors d'oeuvre off the tray of a passing waiter and popped it into his mouth, then followed Frank and Joe to their seats.

Within a few minutes, the crowd was seated facing the plate glass windows that looked out over Manhattan. They were anxiously waiting for Lorenzo to appear. The lights went out and a spotlight lit up the center of the room in front of the windows.

"What you will see tonight should surprise even the most skeptical," Lorenzo's voice intoned from off to the side.

Larissa stepped into a spotlight at the front of the room. The magician's assistant looked radiant tonight, Joe thought. She was dressed in a blue sequined gown, and rhinestone clips held back her long, dark hair.

"Lorenzo is right," she said in a soft whisper. "Magic isn't just about this—"

She reached over to the front row near where Frank, Joe, and Chet were sitting and drew a series of brightly colored silk handkerchiefs from the breast pocket of a man sitting there. The crowd let out an awed sigh.

Larissa smiled and continued. "It's also about—" Dressed in his tuxedo, Lorenzo stepped out into the spotlight in front of the audience. "Illusion."

Joe elbowed his brother. "This guy is too much," he said.

"Shhh!" Chet glared at both of them. "Pay attention!"

Mike Sampson was sitting between his mother and Frank. "Tell your brother to be quiet, please," Mike asked Frank.

"Sorry," Frank whispered, then elbowed Joe back. "Mike wants you to be quiet."

Lorenzo was speaking to the audience again. "For the magician, illusion simply means making your audience see something they think isn't there. Or the opposite."

"Hocus-pocus," Joe whispered. Chet shot him an annoyed look.

"For example," Larissa said. "You think you see lights all over Manhattan. You see them every night—"

"But what if they were to disappear?" Lorenzo asked the crowd.

"Impossible," a man yelled from the crowd. The audience laughed.

"Nothing is impossible," Lorenzo quipped. "I want all of you to concentrate," he told the audience. "Close your eyes. Imagine the city has gone to sleep. There isn't a single light visible for miles around."

Frank decided to go along with the trick. He nudged Joe to shut his eyes, too.

"Now open your eyes," Lorenzo urged.

Frank was stunned by what he saw. Where there had been thousands of lights before, now there were none!

The crowd let out a gasp. "How'd he do it?" several voices asked.

"Illusion," Lorenzo said with determination. He turned to stand with his back to the audience. "Now, while you are looking, I'll make the lights come back on again."

"Sure," Joe said. "What's the trick?"

The magician must have heard him. "No trick," he said from behind his shoulder. "Just illusion."

Frank kept his eyes wide open this time. One by one, as Lorenzo stood there, the lights of Manhattan came back on. The crowd murmured its approval.

"Too much," Mike whispered to Frank. Joe looked stupefied, and Chet sat with his mouth open.

"Tomorrow," Lorenzo concluded, turning to face the audience once again, "we'll go to a magic store, where I hope to show you firsthand some of the props magicians use and how they work. And don't forget the performance in the park tomorrow afternoon."

The group broke up, murmuring its approval of Lorenzo's powers. "How'd he do it?" Chet kept asking as they made their way out of the restaurant and toward the elevators.

"Magic," Mike told him simply.

"Illusion," Joe intoned, imitating Lorenzo's deep voice.

"Right," Frank said. He knew that Joe didn't believe in any of that stuff. "I'm telling you, Joe, if Lorenzo keeps this up, he may make a believer out of you yet."

Frank followed Joe and Chet into the elevator. Katherine Hammond was there, too, along with Irene Sampson and Mike. They were going over the possible ways Lorenzo could have worked his magic.

"Maybe he used mirrors or something," Mike suggested.

"Or hypnosis," Irene offered.

"I don't think so," Joe told them. "He didn't have us concentrating long enough to put us under," he pointed out.

"True," Chet agreed.

The group was quiet for a moment as the elevator made its way to the lobby.

"All I know, Katherine," Irene said sadly, "is that I felt completely underdressed in there. After what happened to me, I'd think twice if I were you about wearing any valuable jewelry."

"You're probably right, Irene," Katherine Hammond drawled in her brassy voice.

Frank glanced over at Katherine Hammond. For some reason, something about the way she looked was different. What was it?

At that same moment, the woman reached up to touch her ear. Then Frank realized what was wrong. Where just before emeralds had been sparkling at Katherine Hammond's ears, now there was nothing.

The thief had struck again!

5 Sleight of Hand

"My earrings!" Katherine Hammond cried out. "They're gone!"

"Not you, too!" Irene Sampson said, turning to her friend.

"Looks like we're back in business, Frank," Joe told his brother under his breath.

The elevator kept going down while Katherine Hammond bent down to search the floor. Mike Sampson got down on his hands and knees and started looking, too.

"What do they look like?" he asked.

Frank described the emerald earrings in the gold settings. "Am I right?" he asked Katherine Hammond.

She nodded. "You've got a good memory," she answered in an emotionless voice.

"I'll bet the thief made off with them when you made me shut my eyes," Joe told Frank.

"That means he—or she—had to be sitting right next to Mrs. Hammond," Chet pointed out.

"Right," Frank said with a nod. "Do you remember if you were still wearing them when Lorenzo made the lights go out?" he asked Katherine.

She shook her head slowly. "The stones were quite small," she said sadly. "I sometimes even forget I have them on."

"Who was sitting on the other side of you, Katherine?" Irene Sampson asked.

"No one," the woman said. "I was on the aisle, remember?"

"As soon as we get to the lobby, Joe and I will head back upstairs," Frank told the group. "We'll search the restaurant and meet you back at the hotel, okay?"

Katherine Hammond nodded. "I should come with you, though."

Once the elevator had stopped at the lobby, Joe held the "open door" button. Chet took charge of Mike and his mother.

"I'll take them back to the hotel," he told the Hardys. "See you in the room?"

Joe nodded. "Right. And wait for us before you report this to the hotel, okay?"

"Why?" Chet asked.

Irene Sampson had a confused look on her face. "Don't you think they should know about this?" she asked.

"We'll handle it," Frank told them. "Nina Bern wants us to keep a low profile on this one, remember? Besides, maybe Spector is still upstairs. We can report the theft to him."

"Do what you think is best," Irene said, taking Mike's hand.

Chet ushered Mrs. Sampson and her son toward the exit. "Good luck, guys," he said to his friends. With a wave, he was off.

"Let's go," Joe said impatiently, pushing the button for the top floor.

"Try to remember what happened," Joe encouraged the woman as they headed back up to the restaurant. "Did you see anyone near you before the lights went out, or afterward?"

Katherine Hammond shook her head. "No. And I didn't feel anyone tug at my earrings, either. But I was paying more attention to Lorenzo than to anything else," she added weakly.

"Whoever is pulling off these stunts is good," Frank said. "He—or she—doesn't leave a trace. Mrs. Sampson didn't notice anything, either."

"Someone's obviously using the magicians as cover," Joe concluded.

The elevator had reached the top floor and was opening now into the restaurant. The room was quiet, except for the noise of the waiters stacking plates and putting glasses into racks.

Lorenzo was off at one side, packing up his gear with the help of a stagehand. When Lorenzo saw Joe, Frank, and Mrs. Hammond coming toward him, he looked surprised.

"Forget something?" he asked.

"Mrs. Hammond lost her earrings," Joe told him. "We thought we'd come back to look for them."

"Not again!" Lorenzo exclaimed. "Why is this happening during my shows?" he asked in a frustrated voice. "Who could be doing this?"

"That's what we want to find out," Frank said. "Is Clyde Spector around?"

Lorenzo shook his head. "He went back to the hotel with Larissa." There was an unmistakable edge in the magician's voice.

Katherine Hammond was searching under the chairs near where she had been sitting. "They're not here," she announced in a thin voice.

"Are you sure?" Frank asked, heading over to help her look.

Joe turned to the magician. "Did you see any-

46

thing suspicious right before the lights went out?" he asked Lorenzo.

Lorenzo thought for a moment. "No. But I think I had my back to the audience at that point. Or did I?" He thought again. "Sorry. I'm drawing a blank. I was concentrating more on the trick than anything else, you understand."

"Try to re-create the scene," Joe prodded. "When everyone in the audience had their eyes closed, was anyone near Mrs. Hammond?"

"I'm sorry, I just can't recall." Lorenzo's stage-hand had finished packing up the magician's gear.

"All set," he told the magician.

"I have to head back to the hotel now, if you don't mind," Lorenzo said to Joe.

"Sure. We'll catch you tomorrow." Joe headed over to where Frank was talking with Katherine Hammond. "Lorenzo didn't see a thing," he told them. "I guess we're not going to find out anything more here, huh?"

Frank shrugged his shoulders. "It doesn't look that way. We should go back to the hotel and let Spector know there's been another theft. It seems like Dietrich is going to have to question some of these guests now."

Katherine Hammond let out a tired sigh. "I think you may be right. I just can't figure out how someone could have done it, though."

"It does take a lot of skill to lift a pair of earrings while you're still wearing them," Joe agreed as they headed back toward the elevators.

"What's that you just said?" Frank asked him. There was a serious look on his face. The elevator doors opened and the three of them stepped inside.

"That it takes a lot of skill—"

"That's it!" Frank exclaimed. "Both thefts happened during the magic shows. Who else besides the audience was at both shows?"

"The stagehands . . . wait a minute," Joe said slowly. "Not the magicians? You don't think—"

Katherine Hammond looked shocked, but Frank smiled slowly. "I know it's a crazy idea, but who else besides magicians could practice the kind of sleight of hand it would take to pull off these thefts?"

"I don't know," Joe said. "You're reaching this time, brother."

"All I know is I'm going to keep a close eye on Lorenzo and Larissa," Frank said with conviction. "What if they really do have something up their sleeves?"

Back at the hotel, Frank and Joe had just finished telling Nina Bern about the most recent theft. The hotel manager was working late in her office, and she didn't look happy to hear the news.

48

She looked even more unhappy when she heard Frank's idea of suspecting the magicians.

"Those two are our draw this weekend," she told Frank and Joe. "They're performing after the gala banquet Saturday night. The guests love them, and anything the guests love, I love, too."

"But—" Joe began.

Nina Bern stood up and smoothed her skirt. "No buts. You can attend their performances and go to their seminars. As for suspecting them of robbery, I think you're way off base."

"I know it sounds crazy," Joe admitted. "Think about it for a minute, though. Even you don't think one of your guests could have committed the robberies. So who else could it be?"

The hotel manager let out an exasperated sigh. "I don't know. A stagehand, perhaps? Someone who just came in off the street to watch Lorenzo perform? For all we know, this whole thing could have been planned a long time ago."

"True," Frank said. "And we'll keep that in mind. Maybe it isn't Lorenzo or Larissa, but you have to admit it's a possibility."

"Anything is a possibility!" Nina Bern exclaimed. She took a deep breath. "Look, I appreciate what you're doing. I know you kids are trying to help, and I want you to keep trying. But don't come in here and tell me my star performers could be crooks. There's too much riding on this."

"Your rating, for example?" Joe asked.

"Exactly. If I cancel Lorenzo and Larissa's performances because you think one of them might be a thief, I stand to lose a lot." She came around her desk and sat on the edge of it.

"So what do you want us to do?" Frank asked.

"You can notify Clyde of what you just told me," she said, standing up and moving toward her door. "Coordinate things with him. Maybe there's another solution you haven't thought of. And maybe, working together, you three can figure it out. But don't—I repeat, don't—let anyone else in on what you've just told me. The last thing I want is for one of the guests to hear that our star magicians are suspected of being thieves."

With that, she opened her door. Joe could tell it was a clear invitation for them to leave. "Okay, Miss Bern," he said politely as he and Frank left. "We'll keep in touch."

Outside Nina Bern's office, Frank let out a long whistle. "That's a tough break. Looks like we're going to have to keep our theories to ourselves from now on."

Joe nodded. "So what else is new?" He started walking down the hall toward the reception desk.

"We should find Spector to break the news," Frank said.

As they walked down the hall, Joe spied a door ajar on their right. He caught a glimpse of a row of small safe-deposit boxes along one wall of the room, then saw a man lean down to open one of the boxes.

Joe recognized the man. "It looks like we have found him, Frank."

Joe slowly approached the door and pushed it open. Inside, Clyde Spector was standing by an open safe-deposit box.

And in his hand was a diamond bracelet!

6 To Catch a Thief

"Hold it right there!" Frank called out.

Spector took one look at the Hardys standing in the doorway and put the bracelet in his pocket. Frank got a good look at it before he did, though —it was a solid band of diamonds half an inch wide.

Suddenly Spector was rushing for the door. Joe grabbed his arm, but Spector twisted out of his grasp and raced from the room.

"After him!" Joe yelled. Frank sprang into action. Spector was already halfway down the hall when Frank heard Nina Bern's voice call out.

"What's going on?" she shouted after them.

"Can't stop to talk!" Frank yelled over his shoulder.

"Hurry up," Joe yelled. He was in front of Frank now, chasing Spector down the hall, toward the door that led to the hotel's registration desk.

Frank tore down the hall, following Joe and Spector past the registration desk and across the lobby. Guests darted in all directions to get out of their way.

"What's he doing?" Frank breathed, catching up to Joe. Spector had charged into the hotel coffee shop.

"Don't know," Joe muttered, "but I don't think we should stop to figure it out."

Frank led the way into the coffee shop. Spector had disappeared into the kitchen. In a few seconds, they were close behind him. Waiters dropped trays loaded with dirty dishes as Frank and Joe chased Clyde through the kitchen.

At the far end of the kitchen, near the pantry, Clyde disappeared down a flight of stairs. In the hallway that led from the staircase, the floor was slippery with grease, and the smell of garbage was overwhelming. Frank had a hard time keeping his footing.

"Whew!" he said, almost choking. "This must be the way to the trash compactor."

Not ten seconds later, they were passing a small

53

room that confirmed his suspicions. A worker was piling trash into a huge metal box.

In front of them, Clyde hadn't slowed down. "He sure does know where he's going," Joe shouted above the noise of the compactor.

"But just where is that?" Frank wondered aloud. His breathing was coming in ragged breaths now. They were chasing Clyde through a maze of tunnels that seemed to run under the entire length of the hotel.

Frank spied Spector turning a corner up ahead. When he and Joe got to the intersection, Frank saw that the tunnel split off in two directions— one to the left, the other to the right.

"Which way?" Joe asked Frank.

Frank listened for a second. Off to the right he heard the distinct sound of footsteps, running hard.

"Follow me!" he called, taking off at a sprint. There was no time to lose. Spector obviously knew where he was going and could use the tunnels to his advantage. Frank and Joe couldn't let too much space come between themselves and Spector.

Then, suddenly, the sound of footsteps stopped. "What the—?" Frank asked. Up ahead, the tunnel seemed to lead to a dead end in the darkness.

Joe slowed to a halt next to him. "What happened?" he asked, taking a deep breath.

"You got me," Frank said, shaking his head in confusion. "I thought we had him. But listen."

Joe was silent. "No footsteps," he confirmed.

"Right. So where'd he go?" Frank started walking slowly toward the end of the tunnel, listening carefully. It was dark enough that Spector might be hiding, waiting to trap both of them.

As he made his way down the tunnel, with Joe following, Frank was more confused than ever. How had Clyde made his escape?

When he got to the end, though, Frank realized what had happened. There was a door hidden in the darkness.

"Clyde must have gone through here," he told his brother. Joe nodded and shoved the door handle.

The door flew open outward. A blast of air greeted them, along with the noise of traffic in the street above.

Frank stepped out into a blind alley. There was no sign of Spector, only old, dirty newspapers swirling around some dented metal garbage cans.

Joe pointed to an iron staircase leading to the street above. "That's probably how Clyde managed to take off," he said.

"He probably planned his escape route," Frank said. "He sure did leave us in the dust."

"He must know the layout pretty well from working here," Joe said.

Frank nodded. "I guess you're right. Well, since we've lost him, we may as well head back inside the hotel. This place is giving me the creeps."

"Me, too," Joe agreed. He led the way up the metal staircase. When Frank emerged onto the street level next to his brother, he saw they were on a side street around the corner from the front of the hotel. He led the way back to the hotel's main entrance.

"I guess this makes Spector more of a suspect than Lorenzo or Larissa," Joe said to his brother.

Frank thought for a moment. Before, it had seemed that either magician could have been responsible for the thefts. But catching Clyde with a bracelet that could very well be Irene Sampson's seemed to kill that theory.

"Possibly," he admitted as he and Joe went through the hotel's revolving doors and headed through the lobby. "Unless he's working with one or both of the magicians."

"True," said Joe. "Hey." He paused for a minute. "I just thought of something. Remember when Mrs. Sampson's bracelet was stolen?"

Frank nodded.

"Just afterward, I saw Clyde talking to Larissa."

"And?" Frank asked.

"And when I was stuck in those trick handcuffs, Clyde didn't know they came from Lorenzo's

56

show that afternoon. He claimed he'd missed it, remember?"

"Hmm," Frank said. "You're right. What if he was covering for himself? There could be a connection. We should keep an eye on Larissa."

"Meanwhile, Nina Bern really should know about this," Joe said firmly.

"You read my mind." Frank laughed. He led the way to the registration desk. George, the clerk, recognized them and let them through the door that led to the hotel manager's office.

Nina Bern was already heading down the hallway from her office. Nat Dietrich was at her side, and he didn't look happy.

"Just what was that all about?" the hotel manager wanted to know. "Why were you chasing my security guard all through the hotel?" She was barely managing to hide the anger in her voice.

"I'll have you know—" Joe began hotly. Frank put his hand on his brother's arm.

"We caught Spector breaking into one of the safe-deposit boxes," he explained calmly, shooting his brother a look.

"You're kidding!" Dietrich exclaimed.

Nina Bern's face turned as red as her suit. "Clyde? Breaking in?" she said in a whisper. "I don't believe it!"

"Believe it," Joe told her. "And that's not all.

57

Your security guard was also holding onto a diamond bracelet. We don't know for sure if it was Irene Sampson's, but I'll bet you anything it was."

"We'll have to look into this," Dietrich said, obviously embarrassed. "You don't think—"

"He's the thief?" Joe asked, finishing the sentence for him.

Dietrich looked more than uncomfortable at the thought. "Well . . ."

"It's possible, Miss Bern," Frank told the hotel manager. "Maybe Clyde will show up and explain himself. If not, I say we run a check on him. I don't want to jump to any false conclusions."

"I think we should take a look at those boxes, too," Joe said.

"As long as you don't touch anything," Dietrich warned them. "I want the police to investigate this thoroughly."

He led them to the room where the safe-deposit boxes were, along with the hotel safe. Nina Bern stood in the doorway while Frank and Joe checked out the room. Nothing seemed to be disturbed. None of the locks on the boxes looked as though they had been picked, either.

"He must have used his own key," Frank concluded.

"There's one thing I don't get," Joe said. "Was he here to take the bracelet out, or to put it back in?"

"It was hard to tell, wasn't it?" Frank agreed. "He could have been using one of the boxes as a drop for the bracelet until he had a chance to get rid of it. We know one thing—he's got the bracelet now, and he's taken off."

"I trust Clyde," Nina Bern said. "There's got to be some kind of explanation."

"Maybe there is," Frank agreed. "In the meantime, my brother and I are still going to watch Lorenzo's performances very carefully to see if the thief strikes again."

Nina Bern nodded slowly. "If this is Clyde's doing, the thefts should stop, right?"

"That would be a logical conclusion," Dietrich said. "If you boys are done in here, though, Miss Bern and I have to get back to work."

"Sure thing," Frank said. "I'm pretty beat anyway. Ready, Joe?"

The younger Hardy nodded. Nat Dietrich and Nina Bern escorted them back down the hall, and Dietrich opened the door for them. "Thanks for your help, boys."

"Hey, Frank, Joe," Chet's voice called out from across the lobby. "What took you so long? I was waiting upstairs forever—oh, hello, Miss Bern, Mr. Dietrich."

Nina and Nat nodded hello. "We'll have the police come and dust the boxes for fingerprints," Nat told them as he was leaving. "Why don't you tell me what the bracelet looked like? I'd like to pay Mrs. Sampson a visit and ask her if it's the same one."

Frank gave Dietrich a brief description of the bracelet. "Would you let me know what she says?" Frank asked.

Dietrich gave his word. He and Nina Bern turned around and walked off, talking quietly between themselves.

"I got hungry," Chet explained. "So I came back downstairs and grabbed a hamburger. What happened?" he asked, looking from one Hardy to the other.

Frank let out a long sigh. "You wouldn't believe it." They told Chet the story as they rode the elevator back up to their room.

"So you really think it's Lorenzo? Or Larissa?" Chet asked incredulously as the elevator opened at their floor.

"Could be, Chet," Frank said wearily.

"But how? I mean, I know how, but why?" Chet didn't seem to want to believe that his idol could be a common thief. The three of them walked out of the elevator and turned the corner. Their room was the last door at the end of a long corridor.

"It happens, Chet," Joe said as he reached for his key. "Sometimes the most impressive looking people are common crooks."

"Allow me." Frank beat his brother to the lock.

He had the key in the door and was turning it when he heard his brother shouting at him.

"Frank!" Joe called out. "Duck!"

Before Frank could make a move, Joe had him in a flying tackle.

"What the—?" Frank looked up from where he was lying on the floor to see a knife come flying through the air.

It buried itself in their door with a sharp *thunk*—right where Frank had been standing scarcely a second earlier!

7 The Knife Thrower

"Frank!" Joe cried again. "Take it easy! I'll be right back."

"What just happened?" Chet asked from the floor. When Joe tackled Frank, Chet went sprawling, too.

"I'll tell you later!" The younger Hardy tore off down the hall. A figure in a black cape and a ski mask was turning the corner and running off in the direction of the elevators.

"Hey, you! Stop!" Joe called out. He took the corner at almost a full run, nearly tripping as he rounded it.

The caped figure was at the elevators now, frantically pushing the buttons. Joe regained his balance and took the fifty feet between him and the assailant at a clip.

"Oh, no, you don't," he cried out in ragged breaths. "You're not getting away from me."

But his words fell on deaf ears, because just as Joe got to the elevators, the doors were closing. All that he caught was a glimpse of the person—who was shorter than he—and a whiff of perfume.

"Rats!" he exclaimed, checking the lights above the elevator door. The car was going down.

Joe searched the hall for the fire stairs. Maybe he could catch the elevator at the lobby.

"That won't work," he told himself a second later. "The guy could get off at any floor between here and there."

As Joe was planning his next move, Chet and Frank came running down the hall.

"Did you get a look at him?" Frank asked. He seemed to have recovered from Joe's tackle.

"No," Joe said. "Sorry, but whoever it was had the jump on me. I can tell you one thing, though. I don't think it was a 'him.'"

Chet looked surprised. "Why not?"

"Because most guys don't wear perfume." Joe told them about the strange scent that lingered after the doors had closed on their assailant.

"Check this out." Frank held out a piece of

paper for Joe to look at. "It came attached to the knife," he explained.

Joe read the note out loud. " 'You may be Hardy boys, but we've got experience on our side. Go home before it's too late.' " Joe laughed. "They've got to be kidding!"

"I think we should take this seriously," Chet said, swallowing hard.

Frank gave a reassuring smile to his friend. "You know this kind of thing happens all the time."

"Sure, sure," Chet said. "And I'm Elvis Presley. I'll bet half the people on this floor get love notes like that one. Whatever happened to the idea of an exciting weekend in the Big Apple?"

"This *is* exciting," Joe told his friend with a crooked grin. "Right, Frank?"

Frank smiled back. "Right, Joe."

"You know what I meant!" Chet exclaimed. He moved away from Frank and Joe. "You guys are hopeless," he muttered under his breath, then started walking toward their room.

"Hey, Chet," Joe said, taking off after him. "All I mean is, we're getting close to finding the thief. That's what this note means. That's what's exciting."

"Yeah?" Chet grumbled. "Well, let me know when the excitement dies down. Otherwise, it might just kill me."

*   *   *

64

The next morning, Joe woke up before his brother or Chet. He lay in bed, trying to fit some of the pieces together in his mind.

"It's no use," he muttered, jumping out of bed and heading for the shower.

"Clyde Spector is working with Larissa." He weighed the possibility as he stood under the shower, soaping himself. "She steals the bracelet, and he offers to stash it for her."

A blast of hot water came through as Joe heard someone in a room above theirs flush the toilet. "Ouch!" he yelled, jumping out of the way.

"What's going on in there?" came his brother's voice through the door.

"Nothing," Joe muttered, turning the water off. He wasn't going to risk getting scalded again.

"I thought maybe our attacker found you in the shower," Frank joked when Joe emerged.

"Very funny," Joe retorted. "Your turn. But watch out for the sound of flushing toilets," he warned.

Chet was just getting out of bed. "What time is it, anyway?"

"Eight o'clock," Joe told him.

"Already!" Chet cried. "I can't believe I slept this late. We've got to get to breakfast. Lorenzo's meeting everyone at the magic store at nine-thirty for a seminar."

"That should give you plenty of time," said Joe

65

as he put on his shoes. "Unless you're planning on eating twice."

"Ha, ha. Hurry up, Frank," Chet shouted through the closed bathroom door.

By eight-fifteen, the three boys were sitting in the hotel coffee shop and had ordered breakfast. "There's Nat Dietrich," Joe remarked, catching sight of the assistant manager talking to one of the waiters. "Mr. Dietrich," he called out.

Nat waved, finished his conversation, and came over to their table. "Mrs. Sampson says she can't be sure from your description if Clyde had her bracelet or not," he said solemnly. "But she thinks it's possible."

Frank nodded and took a sip of juice. "Any word from Clyde?" he asked.

"Not one." Dietrich made a face. "I tend to doubt that young man is going to show up here again. The police dusted the boxes for fingerprints and are going to let us know if anything turns up."

"Good," Joe said. "I'd suggest having someone guard the boxes just in case Clyde comes back, though."

"I'm one step ahead of you," Dietrich said. "Nina was worried because Clyde still has a master key, and it would take a lot of work to change all the locks. If he is a thief, who knows what he might do next."

The waitress brought their meals. Chet dug into

66

his French toast. "This looks great," he said. "Even better than my mom's."

"Well, enjoy your breakfast," Dietrich said. "And let me know if anything develops."

"Sure thing," Joe said as the assistant manager took off.

"Why didn't you tell him about the note you got, and the knife?" Chet asked between bites. "Don't you think he should know?"

"Not necessarily," Frank said. He thought for a moment. "There's not much he can do about it now anyway."

Joe agreed. "Let's wait and see if our mystery knife thrower strikes again." He started in on his fried eggs and home fries. "Hey," he said suddenly. "Knife thrower!"

"Like a magician, you mean?" Frank went on.

"Exactly." Joe paused. "Whoever handled that knife sure did know what he—or she—was doing."

"If you're right about the perfume," Frank concluded, "we're probably talking about a she."

"Wait a minute, you guys," Chet objected. "Now you think Larissa is behind this whole thing?"

The image of Lorenzo's pretty assistant popped into Joe's mind. She didn't seem like the type— she was too soft-spoken and timid—but you never knew. "There's only one way to find out," he said

67

finally. Joe watched his brother, waiting for him to respond.

"We can't confront her about it, Joe," he said eventually. "We don't have any proof."

"True." Joe took another bite of his toast. "Set a trap?" he asked.

"Too risky," Frank replied. "What if it doesn't work? Then the thief will know we're on to him—or her." Frank threw his napkin down on his plate and checked his watch. "It's nearly a quarter of. We'd better go—we have to catch a cab downtown."

Chet rushed to finish his French toast while Frank got up and paid the check. Joe leaned back in his chair and thought some more. What still didn't make any sense was why Clyde was stupid enough to get caught with the bracelet. If he really did steal it, why risk being caught right at the hotel? It didn't add up.

Forty minutes later, Joe, Frank, and Chet walked through the door of Fleisig's Magic Store. The sign claimed that Fleisig's was the biggest magic store in all of New York—and the world.

From the size of the place, that could easily have been true. The huge space was crammed with every kind of magic prop imaginable, from fake blood to a custom box for sawing people in half.

"This place is incredible!" Chet exclaimed.

68

"Maybe we could convince them to open a branch in Bayport."

"Anything's possible, Chet," Frank told him. His eyes were on Lorenzo and Larissa, who were just coming through the store's front door. Lorenzo's normally bright eyes looked a little tired, and his clothes seemed unusually rumpled for someone who seemed to dress so carefully. But Larissa looked fresh and rested in a floral print dress.

The crowd, which had been milling about the store for ten minutes or so as they waited for the magicians, burst into applause.

"Thank you," Lorenzo said, blushing a little. "But this is really your morning."

With that, he and Larissa started the group on a tour of the store. At one end, there were rows of props, including folded handkerchiefs and hats with fake tops. One by one, Lorenzo showed the crowd how to use the props.

Toward the back of the store were the more elaborate magic props. Lorenzo pointed out the trapdoors in boxes that many magicians used to "saw" people in half. He pointed to a special table that had nearly invisible strings attached, which were used to "levitate" a person.

By the store's counter, there was a trick cane that could turn into a flower. Chet asked to see it.

"Wow!" he said, trying it out. "I just have to have this. There's no way you can blow this trick!"

Larissa smiled. "Even the best magicians can make mistakes," she reminded the group. "But he's right. The cane works almost every time."

A short, balding man came out from the back of the store. "Lorenzo!" he shouted, giving the magician a kiss on both cheeks. "I sold this man his first top hat," he told the smiling crowd. "Now look where he is!"

"Alan's right," Lorenzo told the crowd with a grin. "If it weren't for him, I'd still be working in my father's hardware store."

"And who is this beautiful woman?" Alan asked. Lorenzo introduced him to Larissa, and Alan kissed her hand. "So nice to meet you," he said.

After a few minutes, Alan stepped behind the cash register. "Now, can I help someone?" he asked.

Chet held out the cane. "I'd like this, please." He reached for his wallet, then pulled out a bill.

Alan rang up the sale. "I'm sure you'll be quite happy with this," he said as the drawer slid open. "Amateur magicians—" He broke off, staring at the drawer that held the bills.

"Oh, no," Alan moaned. "We've been robbed!"

8 Now You See It, Now You Don't

"There was over five hundred dollars here when we opened the store!" the store owner shouted. "One of you people is a thief!" Alan looked right at Chet.

"I didn't do a thing!" Chet said, backing away from the counter. The rest of the crowd murmured among themselves, and Larissa gave Lorenzo a panicked look.

There were beads of sweat forming on Alan's forehead, and his face was bright red. Frank stepped over and tried to calm him down.

"I'm sure there's some kind of explanation," he said.

"I don't believe this," Joe muttered under his breath. "We've been had—again."

"I know," Frank whispered back. "But let's keep a low profile. Watch the crowd. Make sure no one leaves. We're not going to let the crook get away this time."

"Everyone, keep calm," Joe urged the crowd. "And please," he asked, "don't leave until we find out what happened."

"That's right!" Alan shouted to the crowd. "Nobody move! One of you is a thief!" he repeated. "And I'm going to find out who it is."

Larissa tried to quiet the man down. "Are you sure the register was full?" she asked calmly.

"Of course I'm sure," Alan answered her, raising his arms in frustration. "You people were the first ones here this morning."

"Did anyone else open the register?" Frank asked him. "Someone who works for you?"

Alan let out an exasperated sigh. "I'm alone here in the mornings." He pointed around the store. "There is no one else working with me."

Frank went over the events in his mind. He couldn't remember anyone being near the register while the group took its tour of the store. But maybe he had missed something important.

"How are we going to search all these people?" Joe asked him in a low voice.

72

Frank shook his head slowly. "I'm not sure," he answered slowly. "Chet," he said, turning to his friend. "You were standing by the cash register. Did you see anything?"

Chet furrowed his brow and thought for a moment. "Not that I can remember." He paused for a moment. "Hey, I did see something."

"What?" Joe asked expectantly.

"Well, unless I'm wrong," Chet said in an excited voice, "the drawer was open a little when Alan went to give me my change. Yep, I'm sure of it now."

Alan had gone back to the register and was staring at the empty drawer. "This is just awful," he was muttering. "Who could have done such a thing?"

In answer to his question, Lorenzo spoke up for the first time. "You'll never guess!" he said. His yellowish brown eyes were twinkling in amusement.

What's so funny? Frank was wondering. For someone who was such an old buddy, Lorenzo didn't seem to be treating Alan's predicament very seriously.

"Lorenzo," Larissa said with a slight laugh, obviously catching on. "Did you do what I think you did?"

"Alan thinks he's been robbed by one of you,"

Lorenzo told the crowd, ignoring Larissa's question. "Would anyone here like to confess?"

The group was silent.

"Uh, Lorenzo," Frank said in a small voice. "In my experience, you don't get people to confess by asking them outright."

Lorenzo gave Frank a big smile. "You are, of course, the professional here. But maybe my idea has something to it. Why don't you ask me if I'm the thief?"

"What?" Chet asked, obviously shocked. "Frank would never suspect you of being a thief, would you, Frank?"

The older Hardy stared intently into Lorenzo's strange, yellowish brown eyes. He'd never seen eyes that color before. Looking into Lorenzo's eyes carefully for the first time, Frank realized there was something completely mesmerizing about them.

"No," Frank said finally. "Of course not."

The crowd let out a sigh of relief. Joe nudged his brother. "What's gotten into you?" he asked in a whisper. "That was your big chance. Why didn't you ask him?"

"I don't know, Joe," Frank said, blinking his eyes rapidly. "I think the guy hypnotized me!"

"If Frank had asked me if I stole the money," Lorenzo informed the crowd, "I would have confessed. Because I did!"

He pulled a wad of bills from his inside breast pocket. The crowd gasped in disbelief. Joe let out a cry.

"When you were all paying attention to my touching reunion with Alan here"—Lorenzo handed the bills over to the store owner—"I calmly and quietly opened the register . . ."

"And took the money when Alan was kissing my hand," Larissa concluded, shaking her head in disbelief. "Even I didn't catch it!"

Chet let out a nervous laugh. "You had us all going there for a while, Lorenzo."

"Some student!" Alan said, giving Lorenzo a bear hug. "You even had me going."

"Wow!" a bald-headed man in the crowd said, nudging the older woman standing next to him. Several other members of the group congratulated Lorenzo on his trick and got ready to leave. Lorenzo reminded them about his performance in the park that afternoon with Larissa. "You'll see some exciting things, I guarantee you. I hope you can all make it."

He took Larissa's hand and escorted her out of the store. As Chet went to try again to pay for the trick cane, Frank turned to his brother. "We're going to have to be on our toes more," he said.

"You still think he could have made Irene Sampson's bracelet disappear?" Joe asked.

"Him or Larissa," Frank concluded. "Either one of them is obviously good enough to pull it off."

"So why would they need Spector?" Joe asked. "I've been trying to figure it out all morning."

"Ready?" Chet asked, interrupting their conversation. He was holding on to his cane. "Let's head back to the hotel. I can't wait to work with this."

When they got back to the hotel, Chet went up to the room to practice working with the trick cane. Meanwhile, Frank and Joe sat in the lobby and tried to piece things together.

"What I don't get is why Clyde was trying to hide the bracelet right here in the hotel," Joe asked. "It doesn't make any sense. And if he is the crook, what did he do with Mrs. Hammond's earrings?"

"What if he was trying to return the bracelet?" Frank suggested.

"What?" Joe made a face. "I think that guy really did hypnotize you, Frank. You're not thinking straight. Why not return it to Mrs. Sampson? Why go to all the trouble of putting it in one of the safe-deposit boxes if he intended to let her know he had it?"

Frank shrugged. "I know it sounds crazy."

"Crazy isn't the word for it!" Joe stood up. "I'm going to grab a bite before the show. Coming?"

Frank stretched his legs and stood up, too.

"Sure. Perhaps you're right—maybe Lorenzo did work some magic on me!"

Two hours later, Frank, Joe, and Chet were standing next to a stage that had been set up in Central Park, which was right across the street from the hotel. Frank saw that the crowd was bigger than it had been at Lorenzo's previous performances. Since the stage was outdoors, and it was a Saturday, many people strolling through the park had stopped to see what was going on.

Off at the side, people were lining up at hot dog and ice cream vendors. The hotel had set up a blue-and-white tent at the right of the stage, where there was going to be a small party during the intermission in Lorenzo's show. Frank spotted Irene Sampson and Mike standing between the stage and the tent, and he waved hello.

"Ladies and gentlemen, Lorenzo the Magnificent and the Mysterious Larissa!" a voice cried out over the PA system.

The crowd burst into loud applause. Without any further announcements, Lorenzo and Larissa held hands, took a bow together, and started right in with their routine.

"Watch this one carefully," Chet told Frank and Joe. Larissa was getting into a trunk that was painted in swirling reds and greens. Lorenzo held a long handsaw and spoke to the audience.

77

"I'm now going to perform a most uncomfortable task," he said to the crowd. "Sawing the body of the beautiful and mysterious Larissa in half."

Lorenzo turned the trunk sideways so the crowd could see him perform the trick. Larissa closed her eyes. "Be careful, Lorenzo," she said to the magician.

Frank watched carefully to see if the long legs protruding from the end of the trunk really belonged to Larissa. As if second-guessing him, Lorenzo tickled Larissa's toes, and she laughed.

"Those really are her legs, then," Frank said to Joe. "She's not doubled up inside the top half of the trunk."

Joe nodded and went back to watching Lorenzo. The magician was sawing away while Larissa grimaced as if in pain.

In a few seconds, Lorenzo unlocked the two halves of the trunk. Sure enough, Larissa appeared in two parts. The audience burst into applause.

"Now for the hard part," Lorenzo said. "Putting her back together."

He slammed the two halves of the trunk together, draped it with a blue velvet cloth, and turned it around three times. Then he lifted the cloth and both lids of the trunk. He gave Larissa his hand and she stepped out of the trunk—whole again.

The audience clapped again. Frank shook his

head. "There's got to be a trapdoor or something," he said to Chet.

"Supposedly that's how the trick works," he confirmed. "But I don't see one in the stage."

While Frank, Joe, and Chet were discussing the trick, Lorenzo set up for his next feat. "Since Larissa is such a trusting assistant, she's allowed me to risk throwing these"—he held up a set of knives a stagehand had given him—"right at her."

Larissa smiled weakly and stood in front of a plywood drop at one end of the stage.

Lorenzo went to stand at the other end of the stage. "On the count of three, I'll let go the first knife. Ready, Larissa?"

The beautiful woman smiled again and nodded. "One. Two. Three!"

The knife went hurtling through the air and landed with a sharp sound just above Larissa's right shoulder.

Lorenzo went to throw the second knife. "One. Two. Three!" The second knife landed with another thud over Larissa's other shoulder.

The magician held up the third knife. "Here comes the tricky part. I'm going to aim this knife directly above Larissa's head. Ready?" he asked his assistant again. Larissa nodded.

"One." Lorenzo paused and drew the knife back. "Two." He took aim. "Three!"

But as soon as the magician said "Three," and let go of the knife, Frank had a terrible feeling in the pit of his stomach.

From where he stood, it looked like Lorenzo's throw was off. The knife *was* headed right for Larissa. But this time it wasn't going to miss!

9 The Show Must Go On

At the last second, Larissa ducked. Joe heard Chet let out a cry and saw the knife land right at the spot where Larissa's head had just been.

Joe gasped, but in a second the pretty assistant was picking herself up from the stage. Lorenzo rushed over to her, but before he could reach her, Nat Dietrich was standing over Larissa, helping her up.

"Where'd he come from?" Joe asked his brother.

"You got me," Frank said. "Come on. Let's find out what happened."

With Chet and Frank close behind, Joe pushed his way through the crowd, which was still buzzing from the near-fatal accident.

"Quiet, please," a stagehand was announcing from the onstage microphone. "Everything is fine. Please stay calm." With that, a curtain was pulled, preventing the crowd from seeing what was happening onstage.

Joe pulled himself up onto the stage, found a gap in the curtain, and rushed over to where Nat Dietrich was looking after Larissa. Just as he got there, though, he saw Lorenzo push Dietrich away.

"I thought I told you to leave her alone!" he shouted.

Dietrich threw his hands up in the air. "You don't seem to be able to take very good care of her," he told the magician.

The two men squared off, and Joe was sure Lorenzo was getting ready to throw a punch. Quickly, he stepped between them.

"Take it easy!" he said to Lorenzo. "He was only trying to help."

Larissa's face was a mask of fear. "I'm okay," she managed to say softly. "Please don't hurt each other."

Dietrich reached over and squeezed Larissa's arm. "Take care of yourself," he said. "And you," he added to Lorenzo. "Make sure nothing like this happens again. The hotel can't be responsible for your mistakes!"

With that, the assistant manager walked off the stage. Lorenzo stared after him with his hypnotizing yellowish brown eyes. A look of pure rage crossed his face. He took a deep breath, turned to his assistant, and put a comforting arm around her shoulder.

Out of the corner of his eye, Joe saw Frank motioning to him. His brother was standing with Chet by the plywood backdrop, gingerly holding the knife. Joe went over to them.

"It looks normal enough to me," Frank told his brother. "What do you think happened?"

Joe took the knife from him. "Maybe Lorenzo's concentration was off."

"What are you doing with that?" Lorenzo barked from where he was standing with Larissa. "No one—no one—touches my props."

He let go of Larissa, rushed over, and grabbed the knife from Joe's hand. He took one look at it and started muttering to himself.

"Is something wrong?" Joe asked him.

Lorenzo caught his eye, then went back to examining the knife. "Probably not," he said abruptly.

Larissa was at his side now and was checking out the knife over his shoulder. "Lorenzo, look," she said, pointing at the knife. "Someone carved a

83

nick in the handle. See?" she asked. "Right there."

Joe watched the magician give Larissa a scorching look. "So there is something wrong," he said.

"We can help, you know," Frank put in. "If someone's trying to sabotage the show, we can find out who it is."

"Frank and Joe have been on this case from the beginning," Chet reminded the magicians. "They're trying to find out who's been robbing people during your shows."

"People?" Larissa echoed, giving the boys a worried look. "I thought it was only that one bracelet that was missing."

"Another woman was robbed last night," Joe informed them, almost wishing Chet hadn't blown the case open just now. If one of the magicians was the thief, now they knew he and Frank were watching their moves.

"Who could be doing this?" Lorenzo asked. His angry tone was gone, and now he sounded just plain frustrated. "You really think it's the same person?"

"If it is, it could be someone who's trying to ruin your reputation," Frank suggested.

Joe shot him a questioning look. This was a new theory. Maybe his brother was bluffing. It didn't make sense that the same person who was stealing the jewels was now trying to ruin the magicians' shows. Or did it?

"Let's talk after the show," Lorenzo said finally. "Maybe you're right."

"Fine," Frank said with conviction. "Let's go," he said to Joe and Chet.

The boys left the stage and wandered into the middle of the crowd. People were still talking about what had gone wrong with the trick. One man wondered aloud what was happening to Lorenzo's abilities.

"You don't really believe that someone's trying to ruin their reputation, do you?" Joe asked his brother.

Frank rubbed his chin. "It could be a setup. We have to consider the possibility."

"I don't believe that!" Joe exclaimed. "One of them is working with Spector. They'll probably pull off a big heist tomorrow during that gala benefit," he added.

Chet looked confused. "What makes you say that?" he asked Joe.

"All these people"—Joe pointed out the crowd around them—"are going to be there. Probably wearing their fanciest jewels. And I'll bet you anything that's the moment one of our magician friends has been waiting for!"

"There you go, jumping to conclusions!" Frank

told his brother. "Fact: We still don't know that Clyde helped them steal Mrs. Sampson's bracelet."

"He's right, Joe," Chet said, giving Joe a sideways look.

"Fact," Frank went on. "Someone tampered with that knife. And I doubt very much it was either of them. Larissa could have been killed."

"Wait a minute," Joe said hotly. "Fact: You can't prove the heists are connected to that accident."

Chet watched the two brothers square off. "Do you guys argue a lot when you're on a case?" he joked. "Look"—he pointed to the curtain opening onstage—"Lorenzo's ready to perform. Let's just enjoy the show, okay?"

"You and your facts, Frank," Joe grumbled.

"Chet's right, Joe. There's no point in fighting," Frank said. "Truce?" He held out his hand.

Joe shook it. "Truce. But if it turns out I'm right, you owe me one."

Frank grinned. "It won't be the first time."

"Ladies and gentlemen," Larissa announced. "We appreciate your patience and apologize for that little mishap." She smiled, and Joe found himself laughing along with the rest of the audience. "To make up for it, we're going to give you another chance to watch Lorenzo the Magnificent make his famous, daring escape."

Lorenzo bowed, and the audience cheered. Joe

watched with keen interest as Lorenzo turned to the huge glass tube and started to climb the ladder that was perched next to it. Larissa followed behind.

At the top, Lorenzo sat at the edge of the tube's opening. Larissa locked his ankles into the special cuffs that were attached to a pole that went across the tube's opening. As soon as his ankles were cuffed, Larissa put another set of handcuffs on Lorenzo's wrists and showed the audience that she was pocketing the key.

"Goodbye, Lorenzo," she said, giving him their trademark farewell kiss.

Lorenzo lowered himself head first into the tube, and Larissa closed the top over him. She gingerly stepped down the ladder.

As the tube slowly filled with dry ice vapor, Joe kept his eyes on Lorenzo while Larissa ventured into the audience. This time, instead of pulling rabbits from hats, she made long-stemmed roses appear from out of nowhere.

"She's just too much," Chet said in awe. "Come on, let's get closer." He led Frank and Joe up to the front of the stage.

"Watch how she does it," Chet said. He pointed out Larissa's hand movements as she made a coin appear from the ear of a little boy.

"Sure, Chet," Joe said. His eyes wandered back to the stage. The tube was completely full of vapor by now. He found himself wondering just how Lorenzo managed to get out of his cuffs. He'd have to get his wrists free first, then work on his ankles.

Then, through the heavy mist, Joe saw what he was sure was Lorenzo's face pressed against the inside of the tube.

"Frank," Joe said slowly to his brother, pulling on his sleeve and pointing. "Look."

Frank turned his attention to the stage, too. "What's happening?" he asked.

"I don't know," Joe said, squinting. "But it looks like Lorenzo's in trouble."

The brothers stared at the tube. The mist was thick, so it was hard to tell exactly what was going on. But then Joe spied Lorenzo pounding against the inside of the tube with his shoulder, and he knew he was right.

Something was going very wrong with the magician's trick.

10 False Alarm

"Quick! Do something!" Chet must have seen where Joe was pointing, because he was shouting to Frank and Joe to help out the magician.

Frank pushed his way through the crowd and pulled himself up onto the stage. Larissa was poised at the foot of the ladder. Frank edged past her and climbed the stairs two at a time.

Joe followed quickly behind his brother. A stagehand called out to him, "Hey, kid, you'll need this." He climbed up a few rungs and handed Joe a key. "It's for the cuffs," he explained breathlessly.

Frank was already standing on the platform and prying the top of the tube open with his knife. A burst of dry ice vapor burned his eyes as the tube popped open.

"Rats!" he said, closing his eyes for a second.

"Help me!" he heard Lorenzo cry out. "I . . . can't . . . get out of . . . these—"

"Take it easy," Frank urged, fanning the dry ice out of his eyes. "We're going to help you out."

Joe handed his brother the key. "What's the best way to do this?" he asked Frank.

The older Hardy thought for a moment. The first thing they had to do was get Lorenzo's wrists uncuffed. If he unlocked his ankles first, the magician would plummet head first down into the tube.

"Lorenzo," he called into the tube, "can you hear me?"

"Who is it?" came Lorenzo's muffled voice. "Whoever you are, get me out of this thing— fast."

"Lorenzo," Frank said, "try to lift yourself up. Can you manage that?"

"I'll try," Lorenzo shouted.

Frank heard a grunt as the magician made a move to twist himself around and up.

"It's no use!" Lorenzo shouted after a few seconds. "I can't do it with my hands cuffed!"

Now that the dry ice had cleared, Frank was able to look down into the tube. He saw what the magician was talking about. Without using his hands for leverage, it would be pretty difficult for Lorenzo to pull his head over the level of his stomach.

"We're going to have to pull him out feet first," Joe told his brother.

Frank nodded. "Lorenzo," he called out to the magician, "we're going to unlock your ankles."

"I'll fall!" came the panicked reply.

"We'll hold on to them," Joe shouted. "Trust us."

"I guess I don't have any choice," the magician said in a resigned tone.

"Hold on. Keep still," Joe warned.

While Joe held a tight grip on the magician's ankles, Frank started unlocking the cuffs that held his feet to the pole. For a second, he looked down the ladder to see Larissa and Chet standing there with worried looks on their faces.

"Don't worry," he shouted out to them. "Everything's under control. I hope," he added under his breath as he snapped open the first cuff.

"Got him," Joe reassured his brother as the cuff fell free. "Go ahead with the other one."

"Sure?" Frank asked. The strain on his brother's face was obvious.

"Sure."

"Okay. Here goes." Slowly, Frank opened the lock on the right cuff. He felt Lorenzo's leg jerk free. Joe had the magician by only one leg!

"Grab him!" Joe shouted.

Frank reached for Lorenzo's right leg before Joe could lose his grip on the left one. "Got him!" he said.

"That was close!" Joe said, letting out a deep breath. "On the count of three. One . . . two . . . three!"

Together, Frank and Joe pulled on Lorenzo's legs. "Don't worry," Frank called out between gritted teeth to the magician. "We're going to get you out."

With one more heave, they had the magician halfway out of the tube. Lorenzo managed to pull himself onto the platform. While Joe held his legs, Frank reached out to grab him by the waist.

"There you go," he said when Lorenzo was lying all the way on the platform.

The crowd let out a cheer. "Way to go, Frank and Joe!" Chet shouted from the foot of the ladder.

"I don't know how to thank you," Lorenzo told the two of them as he caught his breath. "I thought it was all over."

"What happened?" Frank wanted to know.

Lorenzo was standing now. "I'd rather not say." His voice still sounded shaky. "Can it wait until another time?"

Frank nodded in understanding. Joe opened his mouth to speak, but Frank interrupted him before he could get a word out. "Lorenzo's just been through a lot. Let him catch his breath."

"Thanks," said the magician. He slowly started to make his way down the ladder.

Frank went to follow him, but Joe pulled him back. "He really doesn't want to talk about it," Joe said to his brother. "Why?"

"Maybe he doesn't want to give away his secret," Frank said. "Or maybe he's finally realized he's in a lot of trouble. Come on, let's see if Larissa is any help."

When Frank got to the foot of the ladder, Chet gave him a big clap on the back. "That was incredible, what you guys did up there."

"Thanks, Chet," Frank said. He looked over to where Larissa was talking to Lorenzo. "How could that have happened?" she was saying. "If you're right, you should fire him. There's no room for that kind of mistake."

"I don't know how it happened," Lorenzo grumbled. "But it did."

Abruptly he walked away from her and went to speak to the audience. "Obviously this isn't our lucky afternoon," he told them. "We're terribly sorry for the mishaps. If you attend our show tomorrow night, we promise they won't happen again. Thank you."

The magician walked offstage, and the curtain was pulled. The show was over.

"Come on," Frank said, turning to Joe, who was standing next to him now. "Let's try to figure out what just happened."

He told Joe and Chet about the conversation he'd heard between the magicians.

"Who's 'him'?" Chet wondered. "A stagehand, maybe?"

"Probably," Joe said. "Maybe one of them botched his job. But how?"

"Let's ask around. Maybe somebody can tell us what could have gone wrong with the trick," said Frank. "Chet, why don't you come with me? We'll find the stagehand who helped out on the trick."

"I'll see if Larissa won't tell me something," Joe offered.

"Good. We'll meet back here in"—Frank looked at his watch—"half an hour."

"Nope," the short, dark-haired stagehand was saying, shaking his head. "I can't tell you. Word of honor." He went back to packing up Lorenzo's gear.

"Cliff," Frank said, reading his security badge. "Think of it this way: We only want to make sure that nothing else happens to Lorenzo."

"Two tricks went wrong today," Chet pointed out. "That's pretty serious."

Cliff looked up from the box he was packing. "I

did my job," he insisted. "Even if he cans me, I know I did my job."

"We know you did, too. So what happened?" Frank waited while Cliff looked around. "We won't tell anyone. That's our word of honor."

Cliff thought for a moment and gave the two of them a long look. "You seem like good kids. I hope you do figure it out. There's a lot of weird stuff going on around here, is all I know."

"We agree," Frank said. He was starting to get frustrated. They weren't getting anywhere.

"There are only two things that could have gone wrong with that trick," Cliff said finally. "One, the locks on Lorenzo's cuffs jammed. Two, Lorenzo had the wrong key. That's all I can tell you."

"What key?" Chet asked. He looked at Frank, who looked at Cliff.

"Yeah," Frank echoed. "What key?"

Cliff shook his head. "Forget it," he said firmly. "That I can't tell you. Look, I've got a lot of work to do." He bent down and picked up a pile of electrical cords. "Just remember the farewell kiss," he added. Then he walked off.

"The farewell kiss?" Chet asked Frank as Cliff disappeared.

Frank shrugged. "I guess that's the secret to their trick. Come on, let's see if Joe found out anything."

Joe was standing by the stage, waiting for them. "Zero," he told them before they could ask. "All Larissa would say is that Lorenzo's been edgy ever since they got to New York."

"And she thinks that's why the trick went wrong?" Chet asked.

"That's what she claimed," Joe said.

"That doesn't tell us much," Frank said. His eyes scanned the stage. "Except that he's got something to worry about."

"Or that Larissa is covering something up," Joe suggested.

"You still think she's the thief, don't you?" Chet asked. "Well, I think you're wrong. I'll bet that when Spector finally shows up, he'll turn out to be the guilty one."

"You may be right," Frank said. "Look, let's get out of here. I wouldn't mind taking another shower after everything that's happened."

"And it's almost time for dinner," Chet added. "It feels like forever since we had lunch."

The three boys walked through the park, where the crowd had thinned out after Lorenzo's show had ended so abruptly. The hotel caterers were packing up their things, and a crew of workmen stood around, getting ready to take down the tent.

"I think we should take it easy tonight," Chet suggested after they had crossed the street and were back inside the hotel's lobby.

"Okay, but we should call Dietrich when we get to the room, to see if there's any news," Joe suggested as Frank led the way to the elevators.

"I'd like to find Irene Sampson later, too," Frank said when the elevator doors opened at their floor, "to see if she can give us a detailed description of her bracelet."

As they walked down the hall to their room, Frank sniffed the air. "Do either of you smell smoke?" he asked.

Chet shrugged. "Not me. Joe?"

Joe had his key in the door. "No."

"Listen," said Frank. "Doesn't that sound like a smoke alarm?"

There was a high-pitched, piercing noise coming from one of the rooms.

"I can't tell which room it's coming from," Joe said as he turned the key.

But Frank was convinced the alarm came from their room. "Joe!" he warned. "Hold it! Don't open the door!"

But he was too late. As soon as Joe opened the door, a blast of smoke sent all three of them reeling back into the hall.

Their room was on fire!

11 Where There's Smoke, There's Fire

Joe held his arms up to protect his eyes from the burning smoke. "Keep back," he told Chet and his brother.

Smoke alarms were blaring all down the hall by now. Several guests had opened their doors. "Somebody call the fire department!" a man in a bathrobe shouted.

"We've got to try to put it out!" Joe shouted to Frank and Chet above the noise.

Frank had already grabbed a fire extinguisher from a glass box at their end of the hall. Chet reached out to close the door.

"We can't let it spread," Chet explained.

"What am *I* going to use to fight the fire?" Joe asked, pointing to Frank's fire extinguisher.

Frank looked around. "Look," he said, pointing down the hall to where the corridor turned. "There's another one."

Joe raced down the hall, smashed the box that held the extinguisher, and came back. "Ready," he said.

"Okay," Frank panted. "Here's the plan. When I give you the sign, Chet, throw the door open. Joe and I'll race inside and try to put out the fire."

"Okay." He paused, then looked at Chet. "Now!" he yelled.

Chet turned the knob and pushed the door open. Frank and Joe held their arms over their eyes and made their way inside the room.

"Look!" Joe pointed to the curtains in front of the window. Frank saw small flames licking their way up to the ceiling.

Joe was already aiming his fire extinguisher at the curtains. "The trash can!" he cried out.

While Joe was spraying the curtains with foam, Frank saw that just below the curtains there was a trash can full of burning newspapers.

He rushed over to the trash can and sent a blast of foam into it. With a scorching sound, the burning papers turned to black, smoking embers.

"How's it going in here?" Chet asked. He was

standing in the doorway, and several other guests peered over his shoulder.

"I think we've managed to put it out," Joe told him. "It looks like someone deliberately set this fire."

Chet stepped inside. He walked over to the window, took one look at the pile of scorched newspapers in the trash can, and let out a long whistle. "Wow! Someone really doesn't want us around," he said.

"It's just a threat," Frank pointed out. "Whoever set this fire must have known we wouldn't be here."

"But how'd they get in?" Chet wondered.

Joe was fingering the curtains to make sure the fire really was out. "They could have gotten a key somehow, or picked the lock."

"Who do you think did it?" Chet asked Frank.

The older Hardy sat down on the edge of the bed and rubbed his red eyes. "Like you said, someone who doesn't want us around."

"I think this might explain a thing or two," Joe said, rubbing his fingers together. "Check it out."

Frank and Chet went over to the curtains. "See this powder," Joe said, pointing to the fine white particles that clung to the red drapes.

"That's flash powder!" Chet exclaimed.

"I thought so," Joe said. "It looks like one of our magician friends has struck again."

"Somebody reported a fire?" called a voice from the door. Two firemen were standing in the doorway. One of them had an extinguisher, and the other one was holding an ax.

"It's all right," Frank told them. "We put it out."

One of the firemen looked at the curtains and shook his head slowly. "Good work, kids. I'll let the manager know everything's okay up here." He turned and walked away with his partner.

"The fire had obviously just started when we got here," Frank said.

"That means whoever set it knew we were on our way," Chet concluded.

"Or didn't expect us to come back so soon," Joe said, offering another possibility.

"Is everything okay here?" Nat Dietrich was standing at the doorway now. "My goodness!" he cried, taking one look at the curtains. "Someone said there had been a fire, but I didn't realize it was this serious." He stepped inside the room. "Are you boys all right?"

Frank nodded. "We're fine. But could you send someone up to help us take care of the mess?"

Dietrich nodded his head vigorously. "Of course. And I'll get you three into another room right away."

Fifteen minutes later, Frank, Joe, and Chet had moved their things into a room on the floor above.

101

This one was a lot more luxurious, with two bedrooms and a separate living room.

"Now, this is traveling first class," Joe said, stretching out on one of the beds. Chet sat in a wing chair, watching TV.

The phone rang, and Frank jumped to pick it up. "Everything's fine, Mr. Dietrich," he said into the receiver. "The room's great. I meant to ask you, has there been any word about Clyde Spector?"

Joe watched while his brother was quiet. Frank listened, then looked over at Joe and shook his head. "Well, you'll let us know, right?" He paused. "Thanks again."

When he hung up the phone, Frank sat down on the bed across from Joe's. "The police still haven't been able to find Spector," he told his brother.

"I'll bet it's Larissa," Joe murmured.

"You mean she set the fire?" Chet asked, looking up from a commercial.

"Think about it." Joe sat up. "The person used flash powder. Only someone connected with the magic show could have done that. We saw Larissa with Spector. He's still missing, but we haven't given up the case. Larissa knows that and is trying to scare us off."

"What about those tricks going wrong earlier today?" Frank asked. "She wouldn't be doing that, too."

Joe thought for a moment. "What if she thinks

102

Lorenzo is on to her? Maybe the magician suspects she's the one who's been taking the jewels."

"But Larissa almost got killed out there!" Chet said loudly.

"What if that was just a smoke screen for Lorenzo's trick going wrong?" Joe wondered aloud.

"That's a little farfetched, Joe," Frank said to his brother.

The phone rang again, and Joe sprang for it this time, making a face. "Popular, aren't we?" he said as he picked up the receiver.

"Joe?" a voice asked.

"Yes."

"This is Irene Sampson. I was wondering, if you and your friends aren't doing anything tonight, would you mind watching Mike for me?"

Joe covered the receiver. "It's Mrs. Sampson. She wants to know if we can baby-sit."

Chet laughed. "Sure. We can order room service and watch a movie. Frank?"

Frank shrugged. "Why not."

"Sure, Mrs. Sampson. Bring him up. Room 1410."

Ten minutes later there was a knock at the door. Joe opened it. Irene Sampson stood there with Mrs. Hammond and Mike. "I really appreciate this," she told them.

"No problem," Joe said. "We were going to

103

spend the night here, anyway." He let them into the room.

Mike gave him an embarrassed grin. "I told my mom I'm too old for baby-sitters, but you guys are more than that really, so I said okay."

Frank laughed. "Mrs. Sampson," he said, turning to Mike's mom, "I know you have already talked to Nat Dietrich, but I wanted to ask you to describe your bracelet for me."

Irene Sampson sighed and exchanged a look with Katherine Hammond. "It's a band of diamonds about half an inch wide. From what Mr. Dietrich said, the bracelet you saw Clyde Spector holding could have been mine, but there's no real way of knowing."

Frank ran his hands through his hair. "I wish we could be sure."

"The only way for that to happen is to find that crook!" Katherine Hammond exclaimed. "Until they do, I'm not even keeping my jewels in my room. I told Irene, too, that she should keep them in the hotel safe or in the safe-deposit boxes. Nina Bern assured me they're being guarded, at least."

Irene reached out and put her hand on her friend's arm. "We should stay calm, Katherine. I'm sure the hotel's doing everything it can." She turned back to Joe. "Thanks again. We'll pick Mike up at eleven if that's okay."

"Sure," Joe told her. "Come on, Mike," he said. "What movie do you want to watch?"

After breakfast the next morning, Frank, Joe, and Chet went upstairs to the banquet room, where Lorenzo was performing with Larissa. It was going to be a short seminar, at which the two magicians would let some of the people in the small group watching take part in the act.

Joe had arranged with the magicians for the three friends to be allowed backstage. "I want to keep as close an eye as possible on these two," he explained to Frank and Chet. They were standing in the right wing of the stage, shielded from the onlookers by a curtain.

The magicians' routine began with Larissa's "disappearing woman" act. Larissa stepped inside a trunk, Lorenzo closed the trunk and draped a cloth over it. He knocked three times, lifted the cloth and opened the trunk. It was empty!

As the audience clapped, Joe looked carefully. He couldn't tell if Larissa had disappeared under a trapdoor or was somehow still onstage and hidden from view.

"What are we looking for?" Chet whispered.

Frank held his finger to his mouth. "Anything out of the ordinary," he said. "We need to make sure that if anything happens, we can account for both Lorenzo and Larissa."

With a flourish, Lorenzo was lifting the cloth off the trunk once again. He rapped three times on the trunk and lifted the lid. This time, Larissa appeared from inside it.

After the applause had died down, Lorenzo asked for a member of the audience to volunteer for the next trick. "I'd like one of you to offer to get sawed in half!" he joked.

The audience laughed, but no one volunteered. Chet pushed Joe out onto the stage. "Go ahead," he urged his friend. "Tell us what it's like."

"I don't know," Joe said with hesitation.

"It'll be fun," Frank urged, pushing his brother onstage.

"Ah! We have a volunteer," Lorenzo announced, pulling Joe center stage. "It's a very simple trick. No need to worry at all."

Lorenzo took Joe aside and explained how the trick worked. It sounded easy enough. All Joe had to do was use his hands to open a trapdoor inside the top half of the box and, when Lorenzo signaled him, double up his legs and swing them through the trapdoor and into a gap in the top of the box.

Joe stretched out inside the box and watched as Lorenzo closed it over him. "Remember to wait for the sign," Lorenzo leaned over to whisper. "When I say, 'You're not ticklish, are you?' that's when you pull your legs up."

Lorenzo locked Joe into the box and picked up a

handsaw. "Joe's a little nervous," he told the group. "But I told him this saw is quite sharp and he won't feel a thing."

The audience laughed uncomfortably. From where he was lying, Joe could see Frank and Chet in the wing. They both had excited looks on their faces.

Lorenzo went to stand at the end of the box. "You're not ticklish, are you?" Lorenzo asked.

That was the signal! Joe reached down to his waist and found the clasps that held the trapdoor in place. All he had to do was get the clasps open and swing his legs through the door and into the gap inside the box.

Joe fumbled with the clasps, trying to get them unlocked. Lorenzo picked up the saw and stepped toward the middle of the box. He had the saw poised and was about to start cutting.

But Joe couldn't get the trapdoor open! He really was about to be sawed in half!

12 Trapped!

"Stop! Stop!" Joe cried out.

Lorenzo held the saw in midair. At first, there was a stunned look on his face, then the magician let out a small smile.

"I told you, Joe," he said. "There's nothing to be afraid of. Just relax."

To his horror, Joe watched as Lorenzo placed the saw over the middle of the box again.

"No!" he shouted again. "You don't understand! I can't get my legs through the trapdoor!" Joe squirmed inside the box. "Let me out of here!"

Lorenzo finally seemed to understand that the trick was going wrong. He put the saw down and

108

started fumbling with the clasps on the outside of the box, trying to get Joe free.

Frank and Chet must have seen what was going on, because they came running from the wing. They helped Lorenzo get Joe out of the box.

"There's been a slight mishap," Joe heard Larissa telling the audience. "I'm afraid we'll have to quit a bit early today, but I hope to see you all at the show tonight."

The curtain came down on the stage. Joe struggled to lift himself out of the box. "That was one tense moment," he said, shaking his head.

"What happened?" Frank asked. "Everything looked like it was going fine."

Joe explained how the trapdoor wouldn't open. "I tried, but the latches wouldn't budge."

Lorenzo was looking inside the box. "I think I've found the problem," he said. "Look at this."

He pointed to the small clasps that held the trapdoor in place.

"Someone nailed them down," Joe said, pointing to two small tacks that kept the clasps in place.

"Let me see," Chet asked. When Joe pointed the tacks out to him, Chet let out a long whistle. "Someone's really trying to mess up your show," he told Lorenzo.

Larissa's eyes clouded over with fear. "This has never happened to us before," she said. "Lorenzo—"

The magician cut her off with a wave of his hand. "Mistakes happen," he said.

"These things are more serious than mistakes," Joe said firmly. "I could have been killed!"

"Or Larissa," Chet said. "She's the one who usually performs the trick."

"Chet's right," Larissa said weakly. "Lorenzo—I'm worried. Do you really think we should perform tonight?"

"You know what they say, Larissa. The show must go on." Lorenzo put his arm around her. "Relax. Maybe it's a New York jinx," he suggested with a small smile. "I'm sure once we've left here, things will start running smoothly again."

"I hope you're right," Larissa said, shaking her head.

"I'm sorry about that mishap, Joe." Lorenzo turned to him and gave him an apologetic smile. "To make it up to you, I'll make sure the three of you have front-row seats tonight. How's that?"

"That would be great!" Chet was beaming.

"Thanks," said Frank.

Cliff, the stagehand, was wheeling the trunk from the stage. "Fix those clasps!" Lorenzo called out as he and Larissa walked offstage. "And I mean it this time: Don't let anyone near any of my props. Do you understand?"

Cliff nodded. "Sure thing," he muttered as he started about his work.

"Did you see anyone near that trunk?" Joe asked Cliff after the magicians had gone.

Cliff shook his head. "Not a soul. Nina Bern and her assistant dropped by, but that was just to check things out—make sure things were set for the gala tonight."

"No one else?" Frank prodded. "You're sure?"

"Of course I'm sure. I know how to do my job," he said.

"Thanks, Cliff," Frank told him.

As the stagehand went back to taking the box apart, Joe turned to his brother. "I know what you're going to say," he admitted.

"What?" Frank asked with a slight smile. "That your whole theory just got blown wide open?"

"What do you mean?" Chet asked.

"Why would Larissa have risked her life just then?" Frank wondered. "Joe thinks the sabotage is Larissa's doing—"

"But she wouldn't have gone so far as to nearly kill herself," Joe finished for him. He made a face. "You're right. It doesn't fit."

"Unless she knew she wasn't going to be the one in that box just now," Chet offered after a few seconds.

Joe looked surprised. "You're right, too!" he said.

"I hate to admit it, Frank," Chet said, "but Joe's

theory still works." He shook his head sadly. "She seems like such a nice person, too."

"I say we confront her," Joe said emphatically. "Before anything else goes wrong."

"Wait a minute," Frank said. "I hate to be a killjoy, but we still don't have any proof. Besides —why would she have taken a nick out of that knife earlier today? You still can't explain why she risked her life that time. Look, tonight's the big banquet. We all agree that if the thief is going to strike again, it's his—or her—golden opportunity. Let's hold out and see if anything happens then."

"Frank! Joe!" a voice called out across the empty banquet hall. "I've been looking for you." Nat Dietrich came rushing across the room. "The police tracked down Spector!" he cried out.

"All right!" Joe exclaimed. "Our big break!"

"There's just one problem," Dietrich said when he came up to the stage.

"What?" Frank wanted to know.

Dietrich raised an eyebrow. "He says he didn't do it."

"You're kidding!" Chet said. "Frank saw him with the bracelet."

"And he was right there the night Katherine Hammond's earrings were stolen," Joe added.

Dietrich shook his head in confusion. "I know, I

know," he said. "I don't see how he can pretend he's not guilty, but from what the police have told me, that's exactly what he's doing."

"I think we should go down to the station," Frank said firmly. He checked his watch. "There's plenty of time before the banquet tonight."

"Actually, the police want to talk to both of you, but not right away." Dietrich looked at his own watch. "They asked me to give them a few hours alone with Spector to see if he confesses."

Joe nodded, then told Dietrich about his near-fatal accident. He explained his theories about Larissa.

"Maybe when we confront Spector with what we suspect, he'll confess he was working with Larissa," Joe told Dietrich as they all walked out of the banquet room.

Dietrich seemed shocked. "You really think Clyde and Larissa were working together?"

Frank gave Joe a look that said he thought his brother had jumped the gun. "It's possible. Joe also seems to think Larissa is planning to pull off a big heist tonight."

"How do you think the accidents fit in?" Dietrich asked.

"If Lorenzo suspects Larissa, she could be trying to scare him off," Joe suggested.

"It could also be a way to keep the audience's

113

attention diverted," Chet said. "If Larissa really is a thief," he added weakly. "I'm still not convinced she is."

Dietrich sighed. "This is all very interesting, and very sad, too. If you're right, the hotel has made a very big mistake in bringing the magicians here."

"We'll just have to keep a close watch tonight," Frank said. "If we can catch her in the act, we'll have the case wrapped up."

Dietrich gave them the address of the police station and told them to wait two hours or so before heading over there. "I hope you boys are right," he told them. "The hotel can't afford another accident. Or another robbery."

"I can't believe he's still pretending to be innocent," Chet said. He was standing in front of the mirror in their hotel room, trying to knot his tie. "How do guys wear these things every day?" he asked in an exasperated voice.

"He's innocent until proven guilty, Chet," Frank reminded his friend. "The police can't make him confess."

The three friends were getting ready for the magicians' gala performance that night. Frank and Joe had spent the afternoon at the police station, giving their statements. Since the police couldn't question Spector until his lawyer was there, Frank and Joe didn't get a chance to talk to him, either, but they did find out that the security guard wouldn't give up his claim of innocence.

"How does he explain what he was doing with Irene Sampson's bracelet? And why he ran away from you?" Chet asked. He'd given up on his tie.

"He won't explain," Joe said in an exasperated voice. "His lawyer was away on business and is flying back now. Until he gets here, Spector won't talk."

Frank picked up Chet's tie. "Allow me," he said with a smile as he began to tie it for him. "We still can't prove a thing," Frank said.

"You keep saying that," Joe said, putting on his jacket. "But when we get a report on that check we asked the police to run on Larissa, we may have the proof we need. And when the word comes in about Spector's record, I'll bet he turns out to be a crook. He's probably holding out on making a confession to protect Larissa until she can pull off the big heist tonight."

"Don't leave Lorenzo out of the picture," Frank said. "The police are doing a check on him, too."

"Why did you ask them to run one on Lorenzo?" Chet asked.

"It was Frank's idea," Joe said. "He thought we should cover all the bases."

"It would be silly not to consider Lorenzo a suspect," Frank said as he picked up the room key and looked at his watch. "If the thief is as good at sleight of hand as we think, it could easily be Lorenzo instead of Larissa."

Downstairs, the banquet hall was set for a fancy sit-down dinner. Crystal glasses shone on the tables, and floral centerpieces gave off a sweet scent. The room was slowly filling up with the hotel's well-dressed patrons. Joe noticed that most of the women had decided not to wear their expensive jewelry. Katherine Hammond was wearing a simple strand of pearls. But even after her recent experience, Irene Sampson had gone ahead and put on a dazzling diamond necklace.

"She's making a big mistake," Joe said, pointing out the woman's necklace to his brother.

"Keep your eyes open," Frank said with a nod in the direction of Larissa and Lorenzo.

The guests took their seats. Frank, Chet, and Joe were at the same table as the magicians. Nina Bern, Nat Dietrich, Irene Sampson, Mike, and Katherine Hammond were there, too.

"I don't like the looks of this," Joe said. "Check Larissa out."

Frank watched the magician's assistant. Her eyes were glued to Irene Sampson's necklace. "I know, I know," Irene Sampson said to Larissa.

"Katherine told me I shouldn't wear it, but Mr. Dietrich said they caught Clyde Spector. I just know that man took my bracelet, and I feel safe now that he's in police custody."

"I hope you haven't made a big mistake," Mrs. Hammond said to her friend, shaking her head.

"I'm sure Mrs. Sampson will be quite safe tonight," said Nina Bern with a reassuring smile.

Lorenzo stood up and tapped a butter knife on the side of a wineglass. "I'd like your attention for just one moment, please."

The dinner crowd hushed, and Lorenzo went on. "As a taste of what is to come tonight, Larissa and I are going to try a new trick."

Larissa spoke up. "Lorenzo's been practicing his powers of levitation."

"What's this all about?" Joe whispered to his brother.

Frank shrugged. "I guess we're about to find out."

The lights in the room dimmed, and a spotlight shone on Larissa.

Lorenzo began to wave his hands over his assistant. "Rise, Larissa, rise!"

To the crowd's delight, the chair Larissa was sitting on slowly rose up from the table. Soon, she was above all their heads.

"Come down, now, Larissa," Lorenzo intoned.

Larissa slowly dropped to the floor. The crowd burst into spontaneous applause and got up to give Lorenzo and Larissa a standing ovation.

"Wow!" Chet cried, on his feet with the rest of them. "That was too much!"

Joe looked around his table. Everyone was standing as the magicians took a bow.

Everyone, that is, except Irene Sampson, who had her hands clutched to her bare throat. There was a shocked look on her face, and Joe quickly figured out why.

The woman's diamond necklace was gone!

13 Illusion!

"We've been suckered again!" Frank heard Joe's voice shouting in his ear.

He looked over at Irene Sampson, who was still speechless, and realized what his brother was talking about.

"Don't anybody move!" Frank shouted above the crowd. "Someone in this room is a thief!"

Chet looked at his friend with a shocked expression. The rest of the guests suddenly got very quiet and started whispering among themselves. Nina Bern swallowed hard and exchanged an embarrassed look with Nat Dietrich.

"Quiet, please!" Nina said, standing up. "Don't panic. Everything is under control."

Frank was keeping a close eye on the magicians. They had both been sitting on one side of Irene Sampson, and that made them both look pretty guilty, even if they had been performing a trick when the necklace was stolen.

"We've got to stop them before they can stash the necklace," Frank whispered to his brother.

"I've been watching Lorenzo," Chet told the Hardys. "It doesn't look like he'd be able to hide it. That is, if he took it."

"The same holds true for Larissa," Joe said, keeping his eye on the magician's assistant.

"There was still that split second when Larissa dropped to the ground after Lorenzo levitated her," Frank recalled in a whisper. "Either one of them could have stolen the necklace and stashed it all at once."

"I'm afraid the dinner this evening will have to be postponed somewhat," Nat Dietrich announced. "I'm going to call the police," he told the Hardys.

"Good idea," Frank said. "Everyone in this room is going to have to be searched," he informed his table, looking at the magicians.

Katherine Hammond was comforting Irene Sampson. The woman still hadn't said a word, and her son was sitting there with a worried look on his face. "I'm sure they'll find your necklace, Mom," he told her. "Won't they, Joe?" he asked.

Joe gave the boy a small smile. "You betcha."

Lorenzo cleared his throat uncomfortably. "I hate to say this, but Larissa and I are going to have to leave. We've got to get ready for the show."

"If you want to search us—" Larissa began.

"I'm afraid we'll have to," Nina Bern told her in an embarrassed voice. "It's to protect ourselves, you understand."

Larissa nodded while Nina Bern took her purse and started going through it. Frank walked around the table to where Lorenzo was standing. "Sorry, but I have to do this."

"I understand," Lorenzo said, smiling down at him with his perfect white teeth.

Frank searched Lorenzo's pockets and patted the magician down. He knew he should wait until the police came, but Lorenzo and Larissa had to leave. They couldn't wait for the police to show up.

Nat Dietrich reappeared after Frank and Nina had finished searching the two magicians. "The police will be here any minute," he reassured Irene Sampson.

"We're going to have to search everyone," Dietrich told Nina.

Nina Bern nodded.

"Will you still want us to perform tonight?" Larissa asked quietly.

121

"Of course we're going to perform," Lorenzo said in a loud voice.

"The show must go on, right?" Joe said.

"That's right, young man," Lorenzo said. "Now, if we're finished here, unfortunately Larissa and I must leave to prepare for our show tonight."

Frank nodded, and the two magicians walked off in the direction of the banquet room next to the dining room where dinner was being served.

"Did you find anything?" Joe whispered to Frank as his brother sat down again.

Frank shook his head. "Not a thing. Look— when the police get here, I think you should stay to watch them search the guests. I'll go back to the room and call our contact at the station."

"You want to know if those background checks have come in yet?" Joe asked, second-guessing his brother.

"Exactly," Frank said as he stood up. "Where should I find you?" he asked.

Joe shot Chet a look. "I think we're going to catch the act tonight, right, Chet?"

"With front-row seats, of course!" Chet said.

When the police started to file in, Nat Dietrich stood up to make an announcement. "The hotel is very sorry, but since there has been a very serious robbery here tonight, we are going to have to search every single guest here."

As the crowd started whispering again, Frank stood up to go. "See you in about an hour then?" he asked.

Joe nodded. Frank walked off and, after being searched by a policeman, headed for his room.

Joe turned to Chet when Frank was out of sight. "I didn't want to say anything with Frank around, but instead of watching while the guests are being searched, I think we should confront Larissa. Now!"

Chet shook his head, looking worried. "I'm not sure that's such a good idea. What if she is the thief? We could be in a lot of trouble."

"Well, I'm going to—with or without you." Joe stood up. "Are you coming or not?"

Chet thought for a moment. "I shouldn't let you go alone. You might get hurt. So, yeah, I'll come."

Joe made his way through the crowd to the exit where Lorenzo had left with Larissa. A policeman stopped him and Chet at the door and searched them.

"You're clean," the officer told them after patting them down. "Go ahead."

Joe led Chet through the empty banquet room and up to the stage where, earlier that day, he'd almost been sawed in half.

"This place is spooky, if you ask me," Chet told him, looking around.

Joe realized his friend was right. The stage was dark except for the footlights, and there wasn't a soul around.

"Where is everyone?" Joe wondered aloud.

Chet shrugged. "You got me. Let's just get this over with."

Joe nodded, and they headed for the backstage area—which was really one long corridor. At either end there were fire exits, and along the way were doors marked with stars.

"This is it," Joe said, pointing to a piece of masking tape with "Larissa" written on it that was stuck to the door.

"Knock!" Chet urged him.

Joe rapped on the door several times, but there was no answer. Finally, he tried the knob. The door was open. Joe gave Chet a questioning look. When his friend shrugged, Joe pushed the door open. There was no one inside.

Joe started looking around the magician's dressing room. He picked up the purse that was lying on Larissa's makeup table and snapped it open.

Inside was Irene Sampson's diamond necklace!

"Chet!" Joe cried out. "Look!"

Just as Joe was about to show his friend what he had found, the door flew open.

Larissa stood there with a shocked expression on her face. "What are you two doing here?" she wanted to know.

"I have a better question," Joe told her. "What are you doing with this?" He held up the diamond necklace.

Chet took in a deep breath. "Oh no," he moaned with a grimace. "She really is the thief!"

"I'm no thief!" Larissa cried.

"You're trying to tell me you didn't steal this?" Joe asked, holding out the necklace.

Larissa shook her head.

"Then how did it get here?" Chet asked.

"I don't know," Larissa said firmly.

One by one, Joe confronted Larissa with his suspicions, and one by one she flatly denied them.

"What were you doing talking to Clyde Spector after your first show?" Joe asked.

Larissa smiled softly. "He wanted my autograph. He said he's a big fan of mine."

Joe and Chet exchanged a look. Was Larissa telling the truth?

"So you're saying you didn't take Irene Sampson's bracelet and give it to Spector? He was seen with it later that night," Joe told her.

"Why on earth would I have done that?" Larissa wanted to know. "I was just as shocked as anyone to find out it was missing. Remember?"

Joe did remember how sympathetic Larissa had been when she'd found out. But maybe it was all an act.

"I saw you looking at Mrs. Sampson's necklace

tonight," Joe told her. Chet looked at the floor uncomfortably. "And now, here it is. Don't you think that's a strange connection?"

Larissa looked him straight in the eye. "I can't pretend I know how that got here," she said, pointing to the necklace, "but I'm not the person you're looking for. And I barely know Clyde Spector."

There was a knock on the door, and they heard Lorenzo's voice. "Larissa. We need you onstage."

"I'm coming," she told him. "Look, I have to go. I hope you believe me."

"We do," Chet offered. "Don't we, Joe?" he asked. Joe was silent. He still wasn't sure. Her answers seemed convincing, but that meant they were no closer to finding the thief. And if she was telling the truth, how did Irene Sampson's necklace mysteriously appear in Larissa's purse?

"While you're trying to find your thief, I wish you'd also figure out why everything is going wrong with the show," Larissa said as she opened the door. "I'm getting pretty nervous, and so is Lorenzo."

"We think there might be a connection, but we're not sure." Joe didn't see any point in telling Larissa he had thought she was sabotaging the show. "We'll let you know if we find out anything."

Larissa smiled. "I can hardly believe you

thought I was a thief, but I guess it makes sense. Still, I've never even stolen a pack of bubble gum!" With a laugh, she closed the door behind her.

"She was nice about it, at least," Chet said, raising an eyebrow.

"Don't say it!" Joe begged. "You think she's telling the truth, don't you?"

Chet started laughing. "You better hope so, or else you just played right into her hand!"

Joe slumped in a nearby chair. "If Larissa wasn't working with Spector, then who was?"

"Lorenzo?" Chet asked, playing with the props on Larissa's makeup table.

Joe shook his head. "Possibly. And maybe he was sabotaging the show because he thought Larissa was on to him?" he wondered, twisting his favorite theory around.

Chet yawned. "Why am I so tired all of a sudden?" he asked. "I can barely keep my eyes open. . . ."

Joe sniffed the air. "Do you smell something?" he asked.

Chet made a face, then yawned again. "Not really."

"Look—" Joe pointed at the door. Small curls of what looked like smoke were drifting into the room from under the door. He raced to the door and pulled it open.

A blast of dry ice swamped him, filling the room

with its fog. His eyes burning, Joe tried to force the vapor away, but it kept on coming. With every gust, Joe felt himself getting dizzier and dizzier.

"Joe!" he heard Chet cry out.

Joe turned to see his friend slump to the floor. Then Joe felt himself falling, too.

"The dry ice!" he thought as he lost consciousness. "It . . . must be . . . poisonous!"

14 Hardy Houdini

Frank Hardy lay stretched out on the bed, waiting for his contact at the police department to come back on the phone. He'd been on hold for ten minutes now, and he was beginning to get more than a little nervous.

"Half an hour until the show," Frank muttered, looking at his watch. Unless he could crack the case, there was no telling what might happen that night.

The thief could strike again. Another trick could go wrong and prove fatal. The crook could make his—or her—escape.

"Come on," Frank said into the dead air. "Let's go."

Frank remembered what Katherine Hammond had said about putting her jewels in the hotel safe, and he felt a little relieved, since it was still being guarded. If only Irene Sampson hadn't tempted fate, she'd still have her necklace now.

His mind wandered to the sabotage that had been happening during the magicians' shows. Somehow he doubted Larissa was behind it—especially since most of the accidents were meant to hurt her. And it couldn't be Spector, since he hadn't been around at all since Frank and Joe had chased him out of the hotel two days ago.

So was it Lorenzo then? And was the magician also responsible for hurling the knife at the Hardys and setting their room on fire? That didn't account for the perfume Joe was sure their attacker had worn. And would Lorenzo have tried to hurt Larissa, too?

"It doesn't make any sense," Frank muttered to himself, checking his watch again. "Come on," he said to the dead air. "I need some answers. Fast."

In Larissa's dressing room, Joe felt himself coming to. His head was throbbing, and his mouth felt like cotton, but at least he was alive.

He struggled to move his hands. Then he realized that his wrists were held behind his back with handcuffs.

130

"Hey, watch what you're doing!" Chet cried out from behind him.

Joe twisted his head and found himself looking right at Chet. They were sitting on the floor, chained together back to back, and there was a huge padlock holding the chain together.

"Don't move," Joe urged him.

"I wasn't planning on going anywhere," Chet said, trying to make a joke.

"Don't make me laugh. My head is killing me," Joe said. He scanned the dressing room. How were they going to get out of this mess? "Can you stand up?" he asked Chet.

"I think so."

"On three. One. Two. Three." Joe heaved himself up off the floor. His legs felt wobbly, but he and Chet had made it. They were standing now.

"Do you have any ideas?" Chet asked. "Or should I plan on spending the rest of my life with you like this?"

"Very funny," Joe said without laughing. His eyes spotted a key on Larissa's makeup table. It just might open their handcuffs.

"Can you help me reach that key?" Joe asked Chet, pointing with his head at the table.

"I think so," Chet said. They turned around and inched their way over to the table.

"Try bending over," Joe told him. They were at

the table now. The key was in sight. All Joe had to do was get a hand on it.

With Chet bent over sideways, Joe had enough slack in the chain to inch his hands along the top of the table toward the key.

"A little more," he urged Chet.

Chet groaned and bent farther in the direction of the key. "How close are you?" he asked Joe. "I can't move much more."

"Almost," Joe said with a groan. He could feel the tip of the key with his fingers. "Got it!" he cried.

"Now what?" Chet asked, standing up straight again and letting out a deep breath.

"We hope it works," Joe said. He held the key with his right hand. "There's no way I can fit this key into the lock on my handcuffs—I can't twist the cuff around. But I might be able to slip it into the one on yours," he told Chet.

Chet nodded. "I was going to suggest that."

Joe felt behind his back for the lock on Chet's right cuff. "Can you see anything?"

Chet twisted his head around. "You're almost there," he told Joe. "A little to the right. There!"

Joe felt the key slip into the lock. He turned it with his fingertips. "Please," he found himself whispering.

With a click, Joe felt the lock snap open!

"Good going!" Chet cried out, pulling his right wrist free of the cuff. "Give me the key."

Joe handed the key to Chet, and within a few seconds Chet's left wrist was free, too. Soon he had used the key to unlock Joe's cuffs as well.

"We're just lucky it was the right key," Joe said with a deep sigh.

"Maybe that's what Cliff meant by the farewell kiss," Chet said.

"What do you mean?" Joe asked.

"Larissa has the key to Lorenzo's cuffs. She passes it to him in her mouth when she kisses him goodbye," Chet explained. "I remember reading Houdini used the same trick with his escape routines."

"You just remembered!" Joe exclaimed.

"I didn't think of it until I saw the key on Larissa's table just now," Chet said, defending himself.

"Wait a minute," Joe said after a moment. "If you're right, that means these cuffs belong to Lorenzo."

"You think he's the one who locked us up like this?" Chet asked.

"None other," Joe concluded. "And that probably means he wants us out of the way for a reason." He looked at the padlock that was still holding the chains in place. "But how on earth are we going to pull off our own escape routine?"

"You think there's another key?" Chet asked hopefully.

Joe scanned the table, but there was nothing there except some makeup and a box of tissues.

"No such luck," he told his friend.

"In that same book on Houdini," Chet said slowly, "there was an explanation of how he managed to slip out of his chains. Maybe we could pull it off."

"There's only one way to find out," Joe said. "What do we do?"

"Well, the book didn't say exactly—" Chet began.

"Can you remember anything, Chet?" Joe could feel his frustration growing. Lorenzo was getting away, and Frank had no idea where they were.

"Houdini let out his breath and sucked in his stomach to create some slack in the chains, then he'd rearrange himself somehow to get more slack. When he got his arm or his leg free, he'd use the extra slack that gave him to untangle the rest of his body from the chains."

"It just might work, Chet," Joe said. "Maybe if we both suck in our stomachs, we'd get enough slack for one of us to get a hand free."

From behind him, Joe felt Chet take a deep breath as he got ready to suck in his stomach. "Ready?" Chet asked.

Joe nodded. As soon as he felt Chet suck in his

stomach, Joe did the same and then tried to pull his arm free. It was no use. He only succeeded in elbowing Chet in the back.

"Ouch!" Chet cried, gasping for air. "Watch what you're doing."

"Sorry," Joe said. "Let's do it again. Maybe it will work this time."

"Can I make a suggestion?" Chet asked.

"Sure," Joe said.

"Don't try to pull your whole arm free," Chet told him. "Just see if you can wriggle your hand out. That will give us some slack to play with."

"Okay, Chet," said Joe. "On three. One, two, three."

Joe felt Chet exhale another breath. Joe sucked in his stomach and wriggled his right hand, gently pulling it up to the level of his waist. He glanced down at his side and saw his hand was almost free.

"Suck in even harder, Chet. We're almost there," Joe panted.

Chet pulled in his stomach even more. Joe twisted his wrist, and his hand came free!

"All right!" Joe shouted.

Chet inhaled deeply. "Wow! I felt like I was turning blue just then."

"We're going to have to do it a few more times before we're really free," Joe said.

It took ten more turns before Joe had his whole arm free, but when he did, there was enough slack in the chains for him to get his other arm free too. Using both hands, Joe was able to get his legs out of the chains. It was only a matter of time before he was completely free and could help Chet get loose too.

"Come on," Joe urged Chet as his friend finished loosening the chains around his stomach. "We've got a thief to catch!"

Frank rushed through the now-empty dining room and into the banquet room where the stage was set up. The police had disappeared, apparently having having finished searching the guests. Lorenzo was talking to Cliff, and Larissa was standing by. But where were Joe and Chet?

Either he'd have to find them, or handle the magician alone.

When he'd finally gotten the information he was looking for from his contact at the station, it was a shock even to Frank. It wasn't Larissa that had the record, but Lorenzo! The magician had been convicted and had served time for safecracking, and his partner in the heist was none other than Nat Dietrich!

No wonder Clyde Spector claimed to be innocent, Frank realized as he plotted his move. He was. And Larissa apparently didn't have anything to do with the thefts either.

Lorenzo was all alone in this, or was working

with Dietrich. Frank still didn't know how the assistant manager fitted in, but he was going to find out.

Slowly, Frank approached the stage. If he could bluff Lorenzo, there would be time before the police returned. He'd told them his suspicions, and several squad cars were on their way back to the hotel.

"Lorenzo!" Frank called out.

The magician looked up from his conversation with Cliff. "Frank!" he said. "I can't talk now. We've got a lot of last-minute things to take care of." He went back to examining the glass tube that was standing on the stage.

"That's okay," Frank said, jumping up onto the stage. "Nat Dietrich wanted me to tell you he needs to see you in his office."

"Really?" Lorenzo asked, looking at Frank carefully. His strange yellowish brown eyes had a suspicious look.

"Yeah," Frank said, keeping his eyes on the magician, searching for some way to stall the beginning of the show until the police showed up. "Something about the police wanting to search this room before the performance starts."

Lorenzo started to move.

"Frank!" Joe called out. He and Chet came running from backstage. "Don't let him get away! He's the thief!"

137

As Lorenzo spotted Joe and Chet running onto the stage, there was a startled look on his face. He grabbed on to the ladder that was leaning against the glass tube. In a flash, the magician had climbed the ladder and was disappearing into the tube.

Frank rushed to follow him. Joe was right behind, and Chet stood at the base of the ladder, holding it steady for the two of them.

"Hurry!" Chet urged.

When Frank got to the top of the tube, the magician had already jumped into it and was standing at the bottom. There was a tired look of resignation on his face.

They had him trapped!

"We've got him!" Frank called out to Joe, who was standing next to him.

Frank looked back down into the tube. But what he saw made his stomach drop.

The magician had disappeared!

15 The Escape Artist

"He's gone!" Frank shouted to Joe.

Joe Hardy peered down into the tube. "Where'd he go?" he asked, turning to his brother.

Frank ran his hands through his hair in frustration. "I don't know, but I'm going to find out."

With that, Frank jumped down into the tube, landing with a crash at the bottom. Joe leaned over the ladder and shouted down to Chet, "We're going after him! Go tell Nina Bern we've caught the thief."

Chet nodded and took off. Joe looked down into the tube and saw Frank motioning to him.

139

"There's a trapdoor here," he shouted. "I'm going through."

"Look out," Joe cried. "I'm coming down."

Frank pressed himself against the side of the tube as Joe jumped down into it. Once he'd landed, Frank lifted the trapdoor.

"So that's how he got away," Joe said, climbing through the trapdoor. "This whole stage is rigged!" he exclaimed.

They were standing underneath the stage, where there was about five feet of clearance. Cables ran under the stage, and in the dim light, Joe spotted several other trapdoors.

"Can you see anything?" Frank asked his brother, crouching down.

Joe spotted a figure about twenty feet away crawling through a jungle of electrical cable. "Over there! It's Lorenzo!" he shouted to his brother.

Frank and Joe took off after Lorenzo. Crouching while they ran made it difficult to keep an eye on the magician, who was crawling under the stage, headed for what looked like a dead end in a far corner.

"We've got him now!" Frank panted.

"Don't be so sure," Joe warned.

As they watched, Lorenzo disappeared into the blackness.

"Not again!" Frank cried.

"I told you not to be so sure," Joe said.

When the Hardys reached the spot where Lorenzo had disappeared, they found another makeshift trapdoor cut into a wall. They scrambled through it and found themselves in the corridor that ran behind the stage.

"That way!" Frank called out, spotting Lorenzo turning a corner just to the right.

They took off after him, spinning around the corner not ten seconds later. In front of them, Lorenzo pushed his way through a fire exit.

"Funny that the alarm didn't go off," Joe remarked as he pushed through the door.

Lorenzo was already on the stairs below them. He took the next flight three steps at a time and pushed open a door at the bottom.

Frank and Joe were right behind him, though, and soon found themselves standing in the middle of the hotel's kitchen. Lorenzo was running past the long row of stoves, headed for the pantry.

As he chased the magician, Joe remembered the layout from when they had chased Clyde Spector. If Lorenzo took the stairs at the end of the pantry, he'd be in the basement, and they'd stand a good chance of catching him—unless he got to the door that led out into the alley before they did.

"Don't stop to think," Frank was urging his brother. "Hurry!"

141

They were following Lorenzo past the pantry now. The stairs were coming up, and Joe assumed he'd follow Lorenzo down them.

Instead, though, the magician went right on running down a long hall.

"Where's he taking us?" Frank asked Joe.

Joe shook his head and kept running. The wide corridor seemed to go on for several hundred feet, and Lorenzo was getting away.

"This guy is fast!" Joe yelled to his brother. "We've got to find some way to trip him up!"

There was a turn coming up. Frank and Joe took it so fast, they almost collided against the wall.

And Lorenzo had disappeared again!

"I can't take much more of this," Joe cried out, coming to a full stop.

"He's got to be here somewhere," Frank told his brother. "But where?"

Frank scanned the walls for some sign of another trapdoor. After searching for several seconds, his eyes fell on a seam in the wall. He pounded it and heard a hollow sound.

"Check it out," Frank told his brother. "Think we can get it open?"

Joe nodded. "If he could, we can," he said to his brother. He started tapping lightly on the edges of the doorway. "We just need to hit it in the right place."

"Let me try," Frank suggested. He started rapping along the top, moving from the right side to the left. When he reached the upper corner of the door, it came open with a little sigh.

"Brilliant," Joe said. "Let's go!" Using his fingertips, he gently pulled the door open and stepped through. Frank was right behind him.

They found themselves in the room where the hotel safe was kept, right next to Nina Bern's office. This was the room where Clyde Spector had been caught with the diamond bracelet in his hand.

And standing there were Lorenzo the Magnificent and Nat Dietrich.

The two men were in the middle of an argument and hadn't heard the door open.

"What?" Dietrich cried. "How did they get here?"

"That's what I've been trying to tell you," Lorenzo shouted. "If you'd been quiet for just five seconds, I would have explained. They followed me."

Dietrich gave Lorenzo a scorching look. "Everything's been going wrong around here, and it's all your fault."

"Should we let them argue this one out?" Joe asked his brother. "Or call the police?"

"Police?" Dietrich asked. "Now, you don't want to call the police, do you?"

"Well, actually, I already have," Frank told him.

"I did a little research and found out you two have known each other for quite some time."

Joe looked at his brother with surprise. "When were you going to let me in on this little secret?" he wanted to know.

"Lorenzo's a well-known safecracker," Frank explained.

"*Was*," Lorenzo insisted, playing it cool. "Not anymore."

"Are you sure?" Frank asked. "I was beginning to think that maybe there was a reason why you're both standing here right now."

Dietrich turned bright red. "I don't know what you're talking about!"

"What *are* you talking about?" Joe asked his brother. "I thought Lorenzo was the thief."

Frank nodded, staring at Lorenzo. "He is. But all those little robberies were really just a smoke screen for breaking into this safe after you had dismissed the guard. Weren't they?"

"That's why you had that trapdoor rigged up," Joe said to Lorenzo with the shock of realization. "And why you knew your way here, isn't it?"

Lorenzo didn't answer him. Instead, the magician took a bag of powder from his pocket and ripped it open. He threw it right where Frank and Joe were standing.

Dietrich had caught on before Frank and Joe

could. The assistant manager had a lighted match in his hand.

"No!" Frank called out.

But it was useless. Dietrich had thrown the match onto the powder.

There was a huge explosion as the powder caught on fire. An incredibly bright light filled the room, and the crash from the flash powder going off filled Frank's ears.

The very last thing Frank heard before being knocked off his feet by the force of the explosion was the sound of Lorenzo's triumphant laughter.

16 The Grand Finale

"Hurry!" Joe cried, as he got to his feet.

As the smoke from the explosion disappeared, Joe saw Dietrich and Lorenzo dash from the room through the same hidden door Frank and Joe had used.

Frank picked himself up off the floor. "Are you okay?" he asked his brother.

"I'm fine," Joe assured him. "Come on. We can't let them get away now!"

Joe led the way back through the door. Lorenzo and Dietrich were running down the long, wide corridor that led toward the kitchen.

Frank was running alongside Joe now. They were gaining on Lorenzo and Dietrich.

"We'll have to jump them!" Frank shouted to Joe.

Joe pushed himself harder. He was practically flying now, but there was still a good fifty feet between them and the two thieves.

When Lorenzo and Dietrich got to the end of the hall, they took a turn and headed for the kitchen's pantry. Frank and Joe were right behind them.

Then, Lorenzo and Dietrich took the flight of stairs that led to the basement.

"Follow them!" Joe yelled. He knew where they were headed: the same exit Spector had taken the other day.

"We can't let them get away," Frank cried out.

They were flying past the trash compactor now, down a long hallway smelling of garbage and mildew. Lorenzo and Dietrich still had the edge on them.

"Should we try to head them off?" Frank wondered, pointing to a hallway that intersected up ahead.

Joe shook his head and put on more speed. "We don't know where we're going," he panted. "We'll get lost down here."

Frank nodded and pushed ahead. Lorenzo looked back over his shoulder. When he saw the Hardys were still right behind them, he motioned to Dietrich.

"Follow me!" Joe heard Lorenzo call out to Dietrich.

Lorenzo put on the brakes and turned the corner.

"Where's he going now?" Joe wondered out loud, skidding to a halt as he rounded the corner.

Frank shook his head. "Another exit, maybe?"

Then, before they knew it, Lorenzo had turned around and was running toward them, full speed.

Joe kept running, but braced himself to tackle the magician. Frank was ready to take on Dietrich.

But Lorenzo wasn't slowing down. It's like some weird game of chicken, Joe thought as the distance between him and the magician got shorter and shorter.

Lorenzo kept barreling toward him. Only ten feet between them now. Eight feet. Five.

Joe reached his arms out to grab onto Lorenzo. But at the last moment, the magician put his head down and butted Joe in the stomach. Joe fell to the ground in a heap. Frank was right behind him and tripped over his brother as he fell.

Lorenzo kept right on going. In a flying leap, Dietrich jumped over Frank and Joe.

"Rats!" Joe exclaimed, pulling himself up.

"That was some move," Frank agreed. "We'll get them this time, though."

They took off after Lorenzo and Dietrich. At the

intersection up ahead, the two thieves ran in the direction of the alley rather than heading back to the kitchen the way they'd come.

Frank and Joe put on the speed again. At the end of the long hallway, Joe spotted Lorenzo trying to pry open the door that led to the outside. It was the magician's last chance to make an escape. Dietrich was standing by, nervously trying to help.

"We can do it," Frank urged. He darted ahead of Joe.

There was more than ten feet between Frank and Lorenzo, but the older Hardy took a flying leap at the two men. The force knocked Lorenzo away from the door.

Joe came running up and slammed himself into Dietrich. The man fell to the floor.

"Got him!" Joe yelled.

Frank was still wrestling with Lorenzo on the floor. The magician wasn't giving up easily. Frank had him in a strong hold, but Lorenzo was trying to kick his way out of it.

"You're not going to win this one," Joe told him, pointing to Dietrich. "Your friend's out cold. Why don't you admit you're trapped this time?"

Lorenzo stopped struggling for a moment and glanced over at Dietrich. His yellowish brown eyes searched the hall for some form of escape. But he

149

quickly realized it was hopeless and gave up his fight. Lorenzo the Magnificent was finally trapped.

"I still find it hard to believe," Nina Bern told Chet, the Hardys, and Larissa a little while later. They were sitting in her office, and the police had just taken Lorenzo and Dietrich away.

"It's incredible, isn't it?" Chet said. His tie was loose now, and he was beaming at Frank and Joe.

"For someone who's just had his idol taken away in handcuffs—and real ones this time—you seem pretty happy," Frank joked.

Chet looked embarrassed for a moment. "I'm just glad I was right about Larissa," Chet explained.

Larissa gave Chet a pale smile and was quiet. Frank realized she was probably still in a state of shock after learning that her partner was a criminal.

"I guess I was wrong," Joe said apologetically. "I'm sorry, Larissa. And Frank, I owe you one."

"That's okay, Joe," Frank said, elbowing his brother. "It's not the first time you were wrong about something."

"What I still don't understand is what Clyde was doing when you caught him with Irene Sampson's bracelet," Nina Bern said, a confused look on her face. "It was her bracelet, wasn't it?"

Frank nodded. "It was. Apparently, Clyde finally explained," he said. "The police said he was trying to protect Larissa." Frank turned to Larissa and gave her a look that encouraged her to tell them about it.

Larissa cleared her throat, but still her words came out a bit hushed and uneven at first. "I—I found Mrs. Sampson's bracelet in my dressing room. Since Clyde had introduced himself to me earlier, I knew he was the hotel's security guard, so I thought he was the right person to return the bracelet to. Besides, since I had no idea how it had gotten to my dressing room, I didn't want anyone to think I'd stolen it." She shook her head sadly. "I guess that was a big mistake."

"Not really," Nina Bern said, her businesslike manner dropping for a moment. "Except I wonder why Clyde didn't tell me, or go to the police."

"I suppose Clyde thought he was protecting Larissa by returning it without saying anything," Joe offered.

Frank looked in Larissa's direction. His eyes met her cool gray ones. "When Clyde disappeared, you didn't say anything because you were afraid he'd actually walked off with it, right, Larissa?" Frank asked.

Larissa swallowed. "Especially since Katherine Hammond's earrings had been stolen by then. I guess I was protecting Clyde at that point. Maybe I had a soft spot for him, too. I couldn't believe he was actually the thief."

"When the real thief—Lorenzo—was standing right next to you, using his magic to divert attention," Joe said, shaking his head. "I guess you'd call his robberies sleight-of-hand thefts!"

Chet looked at the Hardys in awe. "You guys are magicians yourselves, putting all of this together. How did you know how to find Lorenzo's record, Frank?"

Joe spoke up for his brother. "He asked the police to do a cross-check on any convicted thieves having an interest in magic. They can do that now, you know. Sure enough, Lorenzo was into magic long before he became a safecracker, but under a different name.

"And long after," Larissa added with a touch of humor. "Too bad he didn't stick to magic. He had quite a career going."

Nina smiled. "Well, I'm just glad it's all over," she said. "To think that Nat was up to all those tricks. Right under my nose."

"He could have done a lot more damage, too," Frank put in. "Once he wanted us off the case, nothing was going to stop him."

"So he was the one who set that fire in our room?" Chet asked. "I don't believe it."

"Believe it," Joe told him. "He confessed to everything. He even threw that knife at us. And it was Dietrich who tried to sabotage Lorenzo's trick in the glass tube. He switched keys backstage at the show so that when Larissa passed Lorenzo the key in their 'farewell kiss,' it was the wrong key."

"Wow!" Chet exclaimed. "He endangered his own partner with that rotten trick!"

Frank nodded and picked up from where Joe had left off. "He also tampered with the knife that almost killed Larissa. *And* he planted the jewelry in Larissa's dressing room after Lorenzo stole it.

"I guess," Frank continued, "that even though Lorenzo was pulling off the little thefts, he had cold feet about the big one—robbing the safe."

"And Dietrich sabotaged Lorenzo's show," Joe added, "to remind Lorenzo that he'd better go ahead with their plan to rob the safe, or else. Dietrich also told Lorenzo he was going to hurt Larissa. That's why she was framed with the jewelry." Joe shook his head.

"Plus," Frank added, "with the thefts occurring at the shows, most of the guests were too scared to wear their jewelry, so they locked the pieces in the hotel's safe. If Dietrich and Lorenzo had pulled off the heist, it would have been a big one!"

"Was this whole thing Dietrich's idea?" Chet asked, unbuttoning his jacket.

Nina Bern looked uncomfortable. "From what the police told me, Nat contacted Lorenzo when he heard he was coming to perform at the hotel. He'd been planning this for a long time. I guess he blackmailed his old partner in crime and convinced him to help him rob the safe. Nat knew about the trapdoor in the safe room, and he knew the best way for Lorenzo to get here from the banquet room."

"Pretty fancy planning, I'd say," Joe admitted. He yawned. "I don't know about you guys, but I'm beat."

"Me too," Frank said, looking at his watch. "It's getting pretty late."

"I just want to thank you for all your help," Nina told the Hardys. "And you, too, Chet. Now that the jewelry has been found and returned, we can all rest easy. I think I'm even going to offer Clyde a job. As my assistant."

Frank, Joe, and Chet burst into laughter. Larissa smiled, stood up, and snapped her fingers in the air. Then, from behind her back, she pulled a bouquet of roses. "For you," she said, handing them to Nina Bern. "As a token of my appreciation."

Nina Bern blushed. "Thank you, Larissa."

Frank and Joe laughed again. Chet turned to his friends, a smile on his lips. "You laugh. All I can say is I'm glad the weekend's over and we can go back to boring old Bayport. Who ever thought a little magic could be so dangerous?"